Maryellen

1954

Taking Off

by Valerie Tripp

⭐ American Girl®

Maryellen's Scrapbook

We went camping here this summer.

Greetings from YELLOWSTONE National Park

At the Alamo, I walked in Davy Crockett's footsteps and got a hat like his.

Yellowstone National Park

Established 1872

Old Faithful shoots 140 feet in the air!

DAYTONA BEACH MORNING JOURNAL

VOL. XXXI-NO. 88   DAYTONA BEACH, FLORIDA, WEDNESDAY, APRIL 13, 1955   PRICE FIVE CENTS

Vaccine On Way To Doctors

Improved Polio Treatment Gets Full Approval

ANN ARBOR, Mich. (AP) – A potent new 1955 model Salk polio vaccine began rolling last night to doctors' offices to end polio's long reign of terror.

The vaccine was officially licensed for public use by the National Institute of Health only hours after it had been found safe, effective and powerful in preventing paralytic polio.

The vaccine in mass tests last year proved its ability to prevent up to 90 percent of cases of paralytic polio. But since then it has been improved, and this new 1955 mechanism, flooding billions of protective antibodies into the bloodstream. It is these antibodies which build a wall between children and paralytic polio.

The soaring, historic

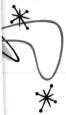

I made my own
birthday invitations.

Help Prevent Polio!
Come to a Show at
Maryellen's House
May 7ᵗʰ, 2:00pm

On July 4, the fireworks
gave me an idea for the
science contest!

Maryellen's Family & Friends

My parents

Joan, 17, and her boyfriend, Jerry

Carolyn is 14, Beverly is 6

Tom is 4 and Mikey is almost 2

Davy lives next door. The boy with the beanie is Wayne the Pain!

The Karens and Angela

TABLE of CONTENTS

A Peek into Maryellen's World

Bridesmaids, Birthdays, and Brainstorms

I n three weeks, I'll be ten!" Maryellen Larkin exclaimed happily. Maryellen and her friends were walking home from school on a sunny April afternoon. Maryellen said, "I've been waiting to be ten my *whole life.*"

"Me, too," said her friends Karen Stohlman, Karen King, and Angela Terlizzi.

"What kind of birthday party are you going to have, Ellie?" asked Karen King, getting down to serious business. "Bowling?"

"No, I did that last year," said Maryellen. "This year I want to do something new—something that no one's ever done before."

"How about a Davy Crockett party?" suggested Karen Stohlman.

Davy Crockett was everyone's favorite TV show. It was about an American hero, Davy Crockett, who lived in the mountains of Tennessee in the eighteen hundreds. All the kids had hats with long fur tails like the one Davy Crockett wore. Maryellen even had "Daisy Crockett" underwear!

"We could sing the TV show theme song," said Karen

Stohlman. She sang: "*Davy, Davy Crockett, king of the wild frontier!*"

"No," said Angela. "We'll sing, '*Ellie, Ellie Larkin, queen of Daytona Beach!*'"

This struck all four girls as hilarious. They laughed until Karen King asked, "Speaking of Davy, will you invite Davy Fenstermacher to your party this year? You have every other year."

"That was back when we were friends," said Maryellen.

Davy Fenstermacher lived next door to the Larkins. He and Maryellen used to be best friends. They'd ride their bikes to school together, eat lunch together, and play together after school and on weekends. But they'd had a falling-out back at the beginning of the school year, and their friendship still was not repaired. Davy never even spoke to Maryellen anymore.

"Davy wouldn't come to my party if I asked him, now," she said. "He's too busy being best friends with Wayne."

"Wayne the Pain," said Karen Stohlman.

Maryellen said briskly, "Ten is too old to have boys at your birthday party anyway. You don't have boys again until you're teenagers in high school, and the boys are your boyfriends, and you play records and dance, sort of like a sock hop only at your house."

All the girls knew that a sock hop was a dance where

you took off your shoes and danced in your socks so
that you wouldn't scuff up the floor. They were trying to
imagine even *wanting* to do such a thing as dance with
a boy, especially one like Wayne, who, they felt certain,
would only be *more* Wayne-ish and pain-ish in high school
than he was now.

"Joan told me about high school parties," Maryellen
added. "That's how I know."

"Ah!" said the girls. They were in awe of Joan,
Maryellen's eldest sister. They respected Joan as their
highest authority on fashion, romance, and being grown-
up. After all, Joan was engaged to her boyfriend, Jerry, who
had been a sailor in the Korean War and was now in college.
Joan and Jerry were already planning their wedding, which
was to take place at the end of the summer. Maryellen was
thrilled, because she was going to be a bridesmaid.

Suddenly, she gasped. "I've just had a brainstorm.
What if I have a movie-star birthday party and everyone
comes dressed as her favorite movie star? I could be Debbie
Reynolds and wear my bridesmaid dress."

"A movie-star party!" said Karen Stohlman. "I love that
idea!"

The girls started naming all the most glamorous movie
stars of 1955.

"I'll be Audrey Hepburn," said Angela.

"Dibs on Grace Kelly," said Karen Stohlman.

"I can't decide if I want to be Elizabeth Taylor or Marilyn Monroe," sighed Karen King. "Or maybe I'll be a television star like Lucille Ball from *I Love Lucy.*"

"Maybe I'll be J. Fred Muggs, the chim-panzee!" joked Maryellen. She loped along the sidewalk, swinging her arms as if she were the famous television chimp. "And Scooter could come as Rin Tin Tin or Lassie," she added.

The girls giggled. Scooter was a very nice dog, but far too stout and lazy to be heroic like the dogs on television.

"Oh!" said Maryellen, bouncing on her toes, "now I'm even *more* excited about my birthday!"

"Me, too," said Karen Stohlman. "I bet your bridesmaid dress is gorgeous."

"W-e-l-l," said Maryellen. "It *will* be, when it's finished. Mom's making it."

"Oh," said the girls.

Maryellen knew what they were thinking. They'd all had experiences with their mothers making dresses as part of do-it-yourself crazes. Her friends were too polite to say it, but Maryellen knew they were thinking that dresses made by mothers didn't always turn out very well.

Angela was the first to think of something optimistic to

say. "Since your mom is making it, your dress will fit you perfectly."

"I hope so," joked Maryellen. "Or instead of Debbie Reynolds, the movie star I'll look like will be the scarecrow in *The Wizard of Oz*."

✳ ✳ ✳

"Ellie, honey," sighed Mrs. Larkin. "Stand still."

Maryellen held her breath. She was standing on a chair while Mom pinned the tissue-paper dress pattern onto her. Mom frowned in concentration, and even Maryellen's energetic imagination had to strain to imagine how a dress would emerge from the tissue-paper pattern. Maryellen hadn't told Mom yet that she was counting on wearing her dress to her movie-star birthday party in a few weeks. Adding the pressure of a deadline would put Mom right over the top with nervousness, she could tell.

Mrs. Larkin sighed again, sounding harassed. Joan, the bride-to-be, looked up from her book and said gently, "Mom? You don't have to do this, you know. I'd be just as happy with ready-made bridesmaid dresses bought off the rack from O'Neal's."

"No, no, no," said Mrs. Larkin. She sat back on her heels and dabbed her sweaty forehead with the back of her wrist. "No, I'm determined to make the dresses. Your dad and I were married during the Depression, and so I didn't have any bridesmaids at my wedding, and I was married in a suit—a borrowed suit at that! I want to do for you every-thing that I missed out on, Joanie."

"Jerry and I don't need a big fuss," said Joan. "Just a small wedding is fine with us."

"Nonsense," said Mrs. Larkin. "A girl's wedding day is the most important day in her life! Your father and I want yours to be perfect in every detail: your cake, your flowers, your veil . . ."

Maryellen piped up, "Your hair, your shoes . . ."

"Jerry and I have talked about getting married outdoors, in a garden or a park," said Joan. "So I'll probably wear flats. We don't want to be all stiff and uncomfortable."

"But I was hoping Jerry would wear his dress whites Navy uniform!" said Mom.

"That's so formal," said Joan. "We want our wedding to be relaxed."

"Joan!" said Mom. "Flats? A park? This is your wedding, not a wienie roast. Honestly, sometimes I think I'm more excited about your marriage than you are." Mom took a pin and—*jab!*—used it to pin the paper pattern for the collar onto Maryellen's shoulder.

Maryellen suspected that the collar was backward. But she stayed quiet while Joan said, "No, I'm excited about the *marriage*. I'm thrilled to be marrying Jerry. But to me, marriage is one thing and the wedding is another. The marriage is forever and the wedding is only one day. Jerry and I want our wedding to be beautiful, just not stuffy and fussy."

"It's not stuffy or fussy to do things correctly," said Mom. "I am determined that you and Jerry will have a proper wedding. For heaven's sake, you're such a bookworm that if I left it up to you, you'd probably get married on the steps of the public library."

"And carry books for a bouquet," joked Maryellen.

"Well, I do love books *almost* as much as I love Jerry," Joan said, smiling. "But I promise I won't get married at the library."

Maryellen laughed. She was glad to see Mom laugh as well—even though laughing distracted her so that she pinned the paper pattern for the sash on backward, too.

❊ ❊ ❊

The next day at school, Maryellen's fourth-grade teacher, Mrs. Humphrey, wrote on the blackboard:

Today is Tuesday, April 12, 1955.

"Wayne Philpott," said Mrs. Humphrey without turning around, "if you shoot that rubber band at Maryellen, you and I will be having lunch together the rest of the week."

Davy snatched the rubber band away from Wayne and put it in his desk, and Maryellen crossed her eyes and stuck out her tongue at Wayne over her shoulder. Sometimes she was glad that Mrs. Humphrey seemed to have eyes in the back of her head!

"Boys and girls," said Mrs. Humphrey, facing the class. "Today we're going to go to a special assembly for the whole school in the auditorium. Line up, please."

As Maryellen and her classmates filed into the auditorium, she saw the principal, Mr. Carey, up front fiddling with the dials and rabbit-ears antenna on the TV set to get a clear picture. It seemed to be a news program. When all the students were seated, Mr. Carey turned up the volume very loud. The screen was too little and too far away for Maryellen and the other students to see, but they could hear.

"Ten years ago today, President Franklin Delano Roosevelt died," said the TV newscaster. "Roosevelt could not walk, because he had had polio, a terrible disease that has killed many people, especially children. Three years ago, in 1952, a polio epidemic affected over fifty thousand people in the United States, and killed nearly three thousand.

"But today, Dr. Jonas Salk, at the University of Pittsburgh, announced that he has found a safe and effective vaccine to prevent polio. The whole world is grateful to Dr. Salk, and to the more than one hundred million Americans who contributed money to research for polio prevention. And now, the task before us is to raise public awareness and to raise money to produce and distribute the vaccine."

The TV newscaster went on, but no one heard the rest of the announcement, because the auditorium exploded with cheers. The students and teachers clapped and whistled. A way to prevent polio was very good news indeed.

Maryellen felt someone poke her in the back. It was Davy. He grinned and raised his eyebrows. Then he turned away without saying anything. But Maryellen knew that Davy's grin was a silent, split-second celebration between the two of them. Davy was letting her know that he realized how the news about the polio vaccine meant even more to her than it did to most people, because when Maryellen was younger, she had had polio. She was all better now. Really, the only reminder was that one leg was a tiny bit weaker than the other, and her lungs were extra sensitive to cold.

But Maryellen remembered very well how much polio had hurt. Sometimes in her dreams she had polio again, and the heavy, dark, frightened feeling of being lost in pain and worry came back. With all her heart, she was glad that now, thanks to Dr. Salk, no one else would ever have to know that terrible feeling. And she was glad that even though Davy didn't seem to want to be her friend anymore, he understood how she felt.

Variety

* Chapter 2 *

ell, I can't say that I'm looking forward to getting a shot," said Karen Stohlman as the girls left the auditorium. "I hate shots." She turned to Maryellen and said, "You're a lucky duck, Ellie. You won't have to get a shot because you already had polio."

Maryellen didn't exactly think she was a lucky duck. First of all, she wasn't lucky at all to have had a terrible illness like polio. Second, she actually felt sort of left out because she wouldn't be getting a shot like everybody else. She wanted to be part of something important and historic, something that was going to change the world for the better.

"I won't be getting a shot either," said Carol Turner, another girl in their class. "My mother says vaccinations are dangerous." Carol shivered. "You know, when you get a vaccination, they're putting a dead virus in you."

"Eww!" said Karen King. "Now I'm scared to get the polio shot!"

"Are you kidding?" Maryellen asked in horrified disbelief. "Finally there's a shot to protect you from a really terrible disease that can cripple you or even kill you, and you're afraid to get it?"

Carol shrugged. "I bet a lot of people think the vaccine is dangerous like my mom does, so they won't get a shot."

"But...but..." Maryellen sputtered, stunned speechless with outrage. Just then, she had a brainstorm. She stopped right in the middle of the hallway and announced, "I've decided about my birthday party."

"It's a movie-star party, right?" said Karen Stohlman.

"No," said Maryellen. A movie-star party seemed self-indulgent and frivolous now. She had thought of a way that her birthday could Do Something Important. "We're going to put on a show. And the point of the show will be to encourage people to get a polio shot. We'll charge ten cents admission and send the money to the March of Dimes to help pay for the polio vaccine for poor children."

"That's a great idea!" cheered Angela, and both the Karens agreed.

Maryellen was excited and proud. She had thought of a way to help Dr. Salk fight polio! And she felt certain that she could figure out a way to wear her bridesmaid dress in her show, too.

✳ ✳ ✳

Maryellen's heart fluttered. Today was the first rehearsal of her show!

All the performers—the two Karens and Angela, plus Maryellen's sisters Carolyn and Beverly—were sitting on the driveway facing the carport, just the way the audience would be for the real show. Maryellen's two little brothers, Tom and Mikey, were sitting on the driveway, too, with Scooter between them. The boys had begged and begged to be in "Maryellen's Dr. Salt show," which Tom kept saying no matter how many times she told him the name was Salk, not Salt. Finally, Mom said that Maryellen should let the boys be in the show and keep them out of Mom's hair while she sewed. So Maryellen gave in. She wanted to encourage Mom to sew because the deadline for her brides-maid dress was drawing nearer and nearer.

"Look, everybody!" Maryellen sang out. "I made post-ers to advertise our show." She held up two of her posters. One showed the heads and shoulders of rows and rows of smiling children, and the other showed a giant dime. On the posters, Maryellen had printed, "Stop polio! Get a shot!" Across the bottom, she'd written, "You can help. Come to a show at the Larkins' house on Saturday, May 7, at 2 p.m. 10 cents admission to be donated to the March of Dimes."

"Oooh," said Karen King. "The posters are swell."

"I made three of each kind," said Maryellen proudly.

"Great!" said Carolyn. "We'll put them up all around the neighborhood."

Maryellen went on, "Now I'll read the script out loud, and you can each decide what part you want to play."

"Hurray!" everyone cheered in happy anticipation.

Before Maryellen had read one word, Davy and Wayne appeared from next door. Davy was being pushed from behind by his mother. "Davy wants to be in your little show, Ellie, sweetie," said Mrs. Fenstermacher. "Your mother called me for some sewing advice and told me all about your show, and I thought it was the cutest idea. And I said, 'Davy, you are going to be in Ellie's adorable birthday-party polio show.' He's shy, but he really wants to. Don't you, hon?"

"I guess so," said Davy, with about as much enthusiasm as he'd have for eating a bowl of worms. Maryellen knew he never would have come over on his own.

"Uh, all right," she said. She didn't mind Davy being in the show. In fact, she was glad—except that Wayne would tag along as always.

Mrs. Fenstermacher went inside Maryellen's house to help Mrs. Larkin, and Wayne flung himself onto the driveway. As usual, Wayne was wearing his propeller beanie hat. And as usual, Maryellen wished the propeller would lift Wayne up like a helicopter and carry him far, far away.

Maryellen ignored Wayne and began to read the script she had written. "Fighting Polio. Act One. In Dr. Jonas Salk's laboratory."

Maryellen was so proud of her script that she could practically burst! Her show was a musical. She had written different words to tunes that everyone knew, inspired by the way Angela had changed the words to the *Davy Crockett* theme song. For example, to the tune of "There Was a Farmer Had a Dog, and Bingo Was His Name-o," she had written:

> *There was a very bad disease*
> *And polio was its name-o,*
> *P-O-L-I-O, P-O-L-I-O, P-O-L-I-O*
> *And polio was its name-o.*

That song was in the first act, which was about polio and Dr. Salk discovering the vaccine. The second act was all about encouraging people to get a polio vaccine shot. To the tune of "Old MacDonald Had a Farm," Maryellen had written:

> *Get a shot so you won't catch*
> *Poh-lee, oh-lee, oh!*

In both acts, the narrator did all the talking while actors silently acted out what the narrator was saying. Maryellen was planning to be the narrator herself, of course, so that she could wear her bridesmaid dress.

As she read her script aloud, she couldn't help noticing that Karen King was playing jacks with Beverly, Wayne was putting grass on Karen Stohlman's hair, and Tom and Mikey looked dazed and glazed. Davy was lying with his head on Scooter's back, looking up at the clouds. But Maryellen plowed on. When she finally said, "The End," everyone clapped halfheartedly. Only Wayne clapped hard.

"I'm clapping because I'm so relieved that it's finally over!" Wayne said. "Listening to that show is about as much fun as getting a shot for poh-lee, oh-lee, oh."

"No comments from the peanut gallery, Wayne," said Carolyn. She turned to Maryellen and said kindly, "The show feels too long, but I think it's just that the driveway is too hard to sit on. People will need pillows or beach chairs or something."

"Well, no offense, Ellie," said Karen King, who was not afraid to be blunt, "but I think the play feels too long because it *is* too long. It needs to be shorter or funnier or something, or people won't like it."

"I could make it a *bit* shorter," said Maryellen, trying to be a good sport. "I could cut out some of the songs."

"No!" said Beverly. "The songs are the only good parts."

"Maybe the show just needs more variety," said Angela.

"In fact, a variety show would be better all the way around, if you ask me," said Wayne.

"No one did ask you," said Maryellen crossly. "Mind your own beeswax."

But Karen Stohlman said enthusiastically, "Variety— that's it! Let's put on a variety show, like *The Ed Sullivan Show* on TV. We can each do different acts, like singing and dancing and juggling and magic tricks."

"That would be more fun for the audience," said Carolyn.

"And for us, too," said Karen King, "because we'll get to do what we *like* to do, instead of just being silent dum- mies while the narrator drones on."

"Wait," Maryellen said. She felt as if her show was galloping away from her. "I—"

But Karen Stohlman rose to her toes and did a pirou- ette, saying, "Beverly and I can do ballet."

"I'll play the piano!" offered Carolyn.

"Angela and I can sing," said Karen King.

"You can do rope tricks," Wayne suggested to Davy, "and lasso Scooter!"

Even Tom piped up, "Mikey and I can do a puppet show with our Howdy Doody puppets."

"What'll *I* do?" asked Maryellen. No one heard her, so she said again loudly, "What'll *I* do?"

Everyone was quiet for a moment, trying hard to think of what Maryellen's talent might be. Finally, Davy said, "You're good at talking. Tell jokes or something."

"Like, why did the clown throw the clock out the window?" said Wayne. "Because he wanted to see time fly. Get it?"

"Be quiet, Mr. Helicopter Head," said Maryellen. "I don't want to tell silly jokes. I want to encourage people to get vaccinated, which is serious and important."

"Well, then make a short speech about Jonas Salk," said Carolyn, "and sing one of your songs. Maybe the one about getting vaccinated, the 'poh-lee, oh-lee, oh' song."

"Yes, that would be good!" said Angela brightly.

Maryellen hugged her script close to her chest. All that hard work for nothing! She was sorely disappointed. But it was clear that no one wanted to do the show that she had written. They just wanted to sing and dance and show off. She had no choice; she couldn't do her show all by herself! So she gave in.

"All right," she said. At least she'd get to wear her bridesmaid dress—if Mom finished it.

Show Biz

✳ Chapter 3 ✳

very day after school, everyone in the show came over to the Larkins' house to practice. At least they were *supposed* to be practicing. But really Wayne and Davy just ran around lassoing each other, chased by Tom and Mikey. The ballerinas, Beverly and Karen Stohlman, couldn't agree on who'd do what in their ballet. And Karen King kept changing her mind about what song she and Angela would sing.

"Oh, I've had the most wonderful idea," Karen King said to Angela the afternoon before the show was supposed to go on. "Let's sing 'How Much Is That Doggie in the Window?' We can borrow poodle skirts from Ellie and Karen Stohlman, and Scooter can be the doggie in the window! Won't that be cute?"

"Mm-hmm," said Angela. "Except I don't know the words to that song."

"I do," said Karen King. "It goes like this:

How much is that doggie in the window?
Something, something, waggedy tail.

How much is that doggie in the window?
La la la la doggie's for sale.

"Anyway, sort of like that," Karen King went on breezily. "It'll be easy to learn the words."

"By tomorrow?" asked Maryellen, trying not to sound shrill. "You're going to learn the something, somethings and la la la's by tomorrow? Because that's when the show is. This is our last rehearsal."

"We know," said Karen King with exaggerated calmness. "You don't have to get all huffy about it."

"Also," said Maryellen, "good luck talking Scooter into having a 'waggedy tail' or doing anything you want him to do when you want him to do it." Davy had already given up on lassoing Scooter because Scooter would just lie there like a sack of potatoes. "Davy has to lasso me instead of Scooter."

"Well, if you're going to be Scooter for Davy, you can be a doggie in the window for Karen and me," said Angela. "You could tie Davy's rope around your waist, and swing the end to be the waggedy tail."

"Ohhh-kay," said Maryellen tepidly. Her own part in the show was so small that she was filling in anywhere anyone needed her. She was the boy ballerina, because both Beverly and Karen wanted to wear tutus. And Tom and Mikey liked to move the puppets, but they didn't know what to say, so Maryellen had to make up a story for them to match what the puppets were doing. When it was time to rehearse her own speech and song, she stood in front of the carport and began. "Fighting Polio," she said. "Dr. Jonas Salk—"

"Hey, Ellie," Karen King interrupted. "Aren't you supposed to wear your bridesmaid dress when you make your speech? When'll you have time to change out of your pants?"

Maryellen pushed her hair off her sweaty forehead. "I'll figure something out." She didn't want to admit to herself or to anyone else that the dress still wasn't finished.

"Fighting Polio," Maryellen began again. She was surprised and gratified that everyone was watching for a change. They were even smiling. *Maybe I'm getting better at it*, she thought. *Or maybe they're just finally beginning to appreciate the important things I'm saying.*

Then, out of the corner of her eye, Maryellen caught a movement. She whirled around and found Wayne right behind her. He was wearing toy eyeglasses upside down and had made his hair stick out all over his head so that he looked like a mad scientist from a science-fiction comic book. He had helped himself to two test tubes from her chemistry set and was pouring water from one test tube into another, as if he were Dr. Salk inventing the polio vaccine. With a sinking heart and a flash of indignation, Maryellen realized that Wayne had been behind her hamming it up the whole time, pretending to be Jonas Salk and miming the actions she'd described Dr. Salk doing in her speech.

As Maryellen watched, speechless, Wayne began shooting his squirt gun straight up in the air so that water flew up like a fountain as he sang,

> *Get a shot so you won't catch*
> *Poh-lee, oh-lee, oh!*

"Cut it out, Wayne!" Maryellen ordered. But her voice was lost in the claps and cheers of the other kids.

"Wayne, that was hilarious!" said Karen Stohlman. "You should do that in the real show tomorrow."

"Yes!" said Karen King. "It's a riot! The audience will love it."

"No!" exploded Maryellen. "I don't even want Wayne to *come* to the show much less ruin my act."

"Oh, come on, Ellie," coaxed Angela. "Wayne's funny."

"It's my show and my act and my idea and my party and my birthday," Maryellen said furiously, "so I get to say if Wayne can be in it or not. And I say, he *cannot*. And that's final."

Everyone was stunned into silence. Even Wayne had nothing to say. An odd expression crossed his face, and Maryellen realized that she'd hurt Wayne's feelings. *Good!* she thought. *Now he sees how it feels.*

"Listen, Ellie, people aren't puppets," said Karen King. "You can't just boss us around and make us do what *you* want us to do."

"All right then," said Maryellen. She was fed up. "Do what *you* want. And I will do what *I* want. I quit."

"You can't," wailed Carolyn. "It's *your* party."

"We can't do the show without you," said Davy.

"You should have thought of that before," Maryellen shrugged. "It's too late now." And she flounced off into the house, slamming the door behind her.

✳ ✳ ✳

At dinner that evening, Carolyn and Beverly wouldn't look at Maryellen or speak to her. Tom and Mikey sneaked sideways glances at her as if they were afraid she was still the fierce sourpuss she'd been that afternoon at rehearsal. Maryellen just toyed with her food. The minute dinner was over, she went outside.

After a little while, Dad and Scooter came outside too. "Hi, sport," Dad said. "Want to help wash the car?"

"Sure," said Maryellen. Dad handed her a bucket and a sponge, and she went to work washing the taillights. They were her favorite parts of the station wagon because they reminded her of giant eyes.

"Rather a chilly atmosphere at dinner tonight," said Dad as he untangled the hose. "What's going on?"

"I had a big fight with everybody at rehearsal today," Maryellen said, "and I quit the show. Since it's my show, they can't do it without me, so the whole thing is off."

"Hmm," said Dad. "That's too bad. I guess that means that your birthday party is off, too."

"It's so unfair," said Maryellen indignantly. "I'm getting cheated out of my party, and none of it was my fault. Wayne ruined everything. I wanted the show to say something serious and important about polio, and he just made fun of it." She sighed. "I guess maybe it was a silly idea, anyway. I mean, that my show could really do any good."

Dad squirted the car with the hose for a minute or two, and then he said, "You know, your show sort of reminds me of our bomb shelter."

"It does?" asked Maryellen. "How?" She knew that bomb shelters were places for people to go to in case an atomic bomb fell. At school, there was no bomb shelter, so during air-raid drills, the students knelt under their

desks or crouched in the hallways with their arms crossed over their heads. At home, Dad had made a bomb shelter in a dug-out area underneath their house. Maryellen couldn't see how the bomb shelter was like her polio show at all.

"If an atomic bomb fell on Daytona Beach, it would wipe out everything here," said Dad. "Our bomb shelter would probably be useless. But it's all I can do to try to protect us, so it's worth my effort. And your polio show is worth *your* effort, Ellie, because it's something that you can do. Something is always better than nothing. Trying is always better than giving up, right?"

"So you think I shouldn't cancel the show?" said Maryellen. "Is that what you're saying?"

"Not exactly," said Dad, wringing out his rag. "I'm asking you if the real reason you're canceling the show is that you think it won't do any good."

"Well, partly I'm canceling it because it isn't at all what I wanted it to be," said Maryellen. "I wrote a script, which no one appreciated one bit! They just wanted to show off dancing and singing and lassoing Scooter, and now my part of the show is nothing."

"Ah, your pride is hurt," Dad said gently. "Was the purpose of the show to give you a chance to be a big famous star?"

"No!" said Maryellen. Then she said slowly, "Well, I did

sort of want people to think of me as someone who could make a difference in something important. So I guess I wanted to be a little bit famous. Is that bad?"

"Not at all," said Dad.

"The purpose of the show was to raise money for the March of Dimes and to encourage people to be vaccinated," said Maryellen.

"I see," said Dad. "That *is* a worthwhile purpose." He turned away, picked up the hose, and gave Scooter a hose-shower-bath, which Scooter loved.

Maryellen sighed. In all the disagreement and excitement, she'd forgotten that what was truly important was the reason for the show: to fight polio.

"I think it's too late to uncancel the show now," she said. "I pitched a big fit. Probably no one even wants to do the show with me anymore."

"Maybe," said Dad. "You won't know unless you ask."

Maryellen hesitated. Then she blurted out, "It will be so humiliating. I'll have to call everyone, and apologize, and say that I'm canceling the cancellation, and ask them to come tomorrow."

"Think you can do it?" asked Dad, squirting the hose at her feet so that she had to smile.

"I'll give it a try," she said.

"That's my girl," said Dad. "You know what they say in

show biz: The show must go on." He smiled. "Good luck."

Maryellen took a deep breath. "Here goes nothing."
She walked inside as if she had cement blocks on her feet
instead of wet flip-flops, dreading apologizing to Carolyn
and Beverly. What would she say?

But it turned out to be easy. As soon as Maryellen said
that she was sorry, her sisters hugged her and said they
were glad that the show was not canceled. Tom and Mikey
hadn't understood that the show was off in the first place,
so they reacted calmly to the news that the show was on.
Next Maryellen called Karen Stohlman, who let out a
piercing shriek of joy and forgave her immediately, and
immediately insisted on calling Angela and Karen King
and telling them the good news. Luckily, no one had taken
down any of the posters. So that left only one more thing to
do, one more person she had to tell. *Actually,* she thought,
squaring her shoulders, *two people.*

Who Do We Appreciate?

* Chapter 4 *

I t had been a long time since Maryellen had cut through the hedge between her house and the Fenstermachers'. She felt nervous. Would Davy still want to be in her show?

Through his bedroom window, she could see Davy gluing together pieces of a model airplane. It was reassuring to see that Davy still loved airplanes, as he had back when he and Maryellen were best friends.

Probably Davy wouldn't even remember their secret signal, Maryellen thought sadly. But she tapped on Davy's window anyway: *Tap, tuppety, tap, tap. Tap, **tap.***

Davy flung his window open. "What's up, Doc?" he asked, just like the old days.

"Hey," said Maryellen. "Sorry I was such a pain before. We're going to do the show tomorrow, and I hope you still want to be in it. So, please come if you want to."

"Okay," said Davy without hesitating.

Maryellen felt flooded with relief and gratitude. "Good," she said. "Now, about Wayne. He's a pain, but everyone thinks that he's a funny pain. Do you think if

I call him and say I'm sorry I hurt his feelings that he'll agree to be in the show?"

"Try and stop him," said Davy with a grin.

Maryellen grinned, too, in spite of herself. "Do you know his phone number?"

"Yup," said Davy. "It's 4628. You can remember it by saying four plus six is ten, take away two is eight."

"Or you could say, 'Four! Six! Two! Eight! Who do we appreciate?'" joked Maryellen. And she and Davy both said together, "Wayne!"

"Thank you, Davy," Maryellen said. "See you tomorrow."

"You bet," said Davy. "See you later, alligator."

"In a while, crocodile," Maryellen replied.

As she slipped back through the hedge to her own house, she realized that was the longest conversation she'd had with Davy since their fight back at the beginning of the school year. It was good to know that even if Davy wasn't her best friend anymore, he wasn't her enemy. Maryellen felt as though she had received one really nice birthday present already.

Maryellen made herself go straight to the telephone and dial 4-6-2-8.

Wayne answered. "Philpott's Pizza Parlor," he said. "Want-a-piece-a-pizza-pie?"

"Uh, no," said Maryellen, who knew that Wayne's family didn't really run a pizza parlor; his dad sold refrigerators. "Listen, Wayne, this is Maryellen," she said, all in a rush. "I'm sorry about today. I hope you'll be in the show tomorrow. And, well, I hope you'll do your funny silent act behind me."

"Righto," Wayne said, putting on a fake British accent. "Jolly good. Pip, pip. Spot on."

"Okay, thanks," said Maryellen. "Bye."

"Cheerio," said Wayne.

And that was that. Maryellen wasn't exactly thrilled that Wayne was going to be in the show, but everyone else thought he was funny, and at least he didn't say anything during the performance, so he couldn't do too much harm. At least she hoped not.

❋ ❋ ❋

Although Maryellen was exhausted when she went to bed, she could not fall asleep. Too many ideas and worries and last-minute details and little things she must not forget to do were in her head, as prickly as pins and needles.

Pins and needles . . . Suddenly, Maryellen sat up. There was one big important thing she had almost forgotten: her dress!

Maryellen tiptoed to the living room, which was dark and silent now, and turned on the little light on Mom's sewing machine. She wanted to see how close her dress was to being finished. Gingerly, Maryellen picked up the material. It was recognizable as a dress, but it still needed to be hemmed, the sash needed to be attached, and the collar still looked backward. There was nothing she could do about the collar, but if she taped the hem up and safety-pinned the sash on, she could wear the dress in the show, and as long as she didn't move around too much, it wouldn't fall apart.

Maryellen went to the kitchen to get tape. When she got back to the living room, Joan was there. Joan had one finger stuck between the pages of her book, and she was peering down at Maryellen's dress. She jumped when she saw Maryellen.

"Yikes!" Joan whispered. "You startled me. What are you doing up? Wait, don't tell me. You're going to finish your bridesmaid dress—with tape?"

"Just the hem," said Maryellen quickly, "so I can wear it in the show tomorrow. Mom didn't have time to finish the hem or the sash, probably because she's been so busy with all the other wedding things."

"Oh," groaned Joan. "Mom's knocking herself out over my wedding. I keep telling her that Jerry and I don't want a big deal, but she won't listen. I appreciate the work she's doing, but I wish I could tell her to *stop*."

"You want me to stop?" asked Mom, suddenly appearing from the hallway.

Joan dropped her book and rushed over to hug Mom. "Not everything, of course," she said. "But the things that are too hard and headachy for you to do, *yes.*"

Mom smiled sadly. "I guess making the bridesmaid dresses *is* a headache," she said. "I had better turn that job over to a real seamstress." Mom tilted her head as she looked at Maryellen's dress. "Did I sew that collar on backward, or is it upside down? Ah, well. I'm not very good at sewing, evidently."

"It's all right, Mom," Maryellen reassured her. "You're good at other things."

Joan and Mom laughed, and Mom said, "I guess I got carried away with the details and lost sight of the big picture."

"You know what? I sort of did the same thing about my show, Mom," said Maryellen. "Sometimes it's easy to forget the reason for something and get all twisted up in the details."

"Your show!" said Mom. "Oh dear. What will you wear in your show tomorrow if you can't wear your bridesmaid dress, Ellie?"

"I'll think of something," said Maryellen, hiding her disappointment.

"I know!" said Joan. "How about my pink prom dress? It'll be a little big, but we can pin it, or ..." She smiled at Maryellen, "tape it! It was my very first prom dress. Remember?"

"Of course I remember," said Maryellen. She had a fleeting flash of sorrow; though the pink dress was pretty, it wasn't hers. But she said gratefully, "Thanks, Joan. I'd love to wear it."

"Problem solved," said Mom, hanging Maryellen's unfinished bridesmaid dress on a hanger. "Now can we all please go to bed? Tomorrow is a big day. Birthday girls need their beauty sleep, especially one who's putting on a show."

Mom turned off the little sewing-machine light, and the living room was dark and silent once more. As Joan and Maryellen walked down the hallway to their room, Joan said softly, "You are going to look like a million bucks in that pink prom dress tomorrow, Ell-a-reenie. Wait and see."

✳ ✳ ✳

Maryellen peeked between the two sheets that were serving as curtains to hide backstage, which was really the carport. Quite a good-sized crowd had come to see the show. Mrs. Stohlman, Mrs. King, and Mrs. Fenstermacher sat in beach chairs in the back row, talking with Angela's mother and grandmother. Wayne's parents, Mr. and Mrs.

Philpott, had come, too. Mr. Philpott had a Kodak movie
camera, and he was standing at the end of the
driveway, filming people as they dropped
their dimes into the empty coffee can to
pay their admission. Families from the
neighborhood were there, as well as six
kids from her class at school. Scooter
sashayed from person to person, gra-
ciously allowing everyone to pat him on
the head while he drooled on their laps.

"Scooter!" Maryellen whispered from behind the
curtain. "Come!"

But Scooter just made himself comfortable right in the
middle of the stage, which was really the driveway, and
refused to budge. Maryellen had no choice but to step
over Scooter when she went in front of the curtain to say,
"Welcome to our show." Then she had to step over him
backward when she went behind the curtain again.

Naturally, however, Scooter wandered away when
Angela and Karen King came out in their matching poodle
skirts to sing "How Much Is That Doggie in the Window?"
So Maryellen had to be the dog with the waggedy tail,
swinging Davy's rope behind her. It actually turned out
to be a good thing that she was onstage, because Angela
and Karen King had not learned all the words to the song,

so Maryellen sang really loud when they came to a part they didn't know. The audience clapped and cheered, and Angela and Karen King curtsied and smiled while Maryellen darted backstage, gave Davy his rope, and then came back onstage so that Davy could lasso her. The audience oohed and aahed every time Davy made the rope swoop over his head and then loop around her.

Tom and Mikey's puppet act was next. The little boys were supposed to crouch behind a box and move their puppets around while Maryellen told a story. But Mikey stood up and waved his hand with the puppet on it to the audience. Everyone laughed and clapped and cheered so much that Tom stood up and waved his puppet, too, so Maryellen gave up on telling any story and let the little boys smile and wave until Carolyn began to play the music for Karen Stohlman and Beverly's ballet dance. The music gave Maryellen time to run to her room to change.

Maryellen flew into her bedroom and then screeched to a halt. She couldn't believe her eyes when she saw what was hanging on her closet door. It wasn't the pink prom dress. It was her gorgeous green bridesmaid dress. Finished! Perfect! The hem was hemmed, the sash was attached, and the collar was on the right way. Pinned to the dress was a note:

Dear Ellie,
A darling girl in a darling show deserves her own darling
dress.
Love,
Mrs. Fenstermacher

Maryellen's heart was filled with joy and gratitude as
she slipped the dress over her head. *Mom must have asked*
Mrs. Fenstermacher to finish it this morning, she realized,
while the rest of us were hurrying around getting ready for the
show. She allowed herself one quick glance at herself in the
mirror—oh, the dress was lovely!—and then she had to
race back to the stage. Everything was happening so fast! It
was time for her speech about Jonas Salk, which meant that
the show was nearly over.

Frozen

✳ Chapter 5 ✳

ifting the hem of her skirt gracefully, Maryellen stepped out from between the curtains, and the audience gasped in admiration at the sight of her in the snazzy green dress. Maryellen smiled a special smile at Mrs. Fenstermacher, who waved back.

Maryellen tried to begin her speech, but it came out all squeaky. "Fighting," she said in a tight, high voice. She tried again, "Fighting . . ." She swallowed hard. "Uh . . ."

"Polio!" Karen King whispered loudly, prompting from behind the curtains. "You're supposed to say, 'Fighting Polio.'"

Maryellen knew what she was supposed to say, but somehow she could not. Her mouth was dry. Her legs were as shaky as Jell-O. Her brain was empty. And her heart was thumping wildly. She wished Davy would lasso her and haul her off the stage. What on earth was the matter with her? She should have confidence; wasn't she wearing the most beautiful dress she'd ever worn? And she knew everyone in the audience, for Pete's sake. And yet when she looked at them all waiting for her to speak, she couldn't move a muscle. The only sound was the ominous whirring of Mr. Philpott's movie camera. Unexpectedly, horribly, nightmarishly, Maryellen was frozen with stage fright.

She felt as though she'd been standing there for hours and hours, trembling in agony, unable to speak or move or even breathe, when suddenly Wayne thrust his head out between the curtains. Never in a million years would Maryellen have thought she'd be glad to see Wayne, but she definitely was right now. He looked so funny with his toy eyeglasses on upside down and his hair sticking out all over his head that the audience chuckled. They laughed even more when he pretended to get his feet all tangled up in the curtains as he fought his way onto the stage.

"Hey!" Wayne said to Maryellen. "Do you know who I am?" She could only look at him, wide-eyed, as if she had never seen him before in her life. But it didn't matter, because Wayne chattered on, giving the information that Maryellen was supposed to give but could not. "I'm Dr. Jonas Salk, that's who. And do you know what I invented?"

Maryellen opened her mouth, but nothing came out.

"I invented a vaccine that prevents polio," said Wayne. He turned to the audience. "You all know that polio is a terrible, terrible disease. It hurts millions of people, especially children, and makes them very sick and sometimes they can't ever walk again. Now, at last, after many years of research, I have found a safe vaccine to protect you from polio. So ..." Wayne flung his arms out wide and sang,

> Get a shot so you won't catch
> Poh-lee, oh-lee, oh!

Then he said, "Come on, everybody! All together now!" All the cast members crowded out from behind the curtains. Wayne waved his arms as if he were conducting an orchestra and led them and the audience in singing,

> Get a shot so you won't catch
> Poh-lee, oh-lee, oh!

The audience stood up and cheered. Wayne took exaggerated bows and then rose up on his toes, waving his clasped hands over his head like a winning prizefighter, which made the audience laugh and clap even more.

Maryellen managed to smile at Wayne. It was a weak, watery smile, but it was humble and sincere.

Wayne cheerfully thumped her on the back, and bowed again and again to make the audience keep applauding.

✳ ✳ ✳

After the show, Mom served birthday cake and lemonade. Maryellen, who'd changed out of her dress, was sitting in the shade and eating her cake with Karen King, Angela, and Davy when Karen Stohlman came over.

"Gosh," said Karen Stohlman, "what in the world happened to you, Ellie? You were standing out there on the stage like a mummy."

Maryellen shuddered, remembering. "Stage fright, I guess," she said.

"I thought you were going to faint," said Angela.

"Well, Wayne sure came to your rescue," said Karen Stohlman.

"Wayne saved the whole show," said Karen King.

"Yes," said Maryellen. "I never thought I'd say this, but thank goodness for Wayne!"

Davy grinned and chanted, "Four-six-two-eight! Who do we appreciate?"

And all five kids said, "Wayne!"

"Where is Wayne, by the way?" Maryellen asked.

Davy tilted his head toward the stage. There was Wayne. He had Beverly's tutu on his head and Karen Stohlman's tutu around his waist on top of his pants, and he was imitating the ballet they had danced in the show while his father filmed him.

✳ ✳ ✳

Ching, ching, ching. The dimes made a cheerful jingly sound as Maryellen poured them out of the coffee can

onto the kitchen table. Everyone had gone home, and all the Larkins were sitting in the kitchen Saturday evening while Maryellen counted the money the show had earned.

"So many people came today!" said Beverly as Maryellen added up the dimes.

"I bet we earned twenty-eleven dollars!" said Tom.

Maryellen grinned. "Not quite that much," she said. "We earned three dollars and twenty cents."

"That's a respectable amount," said Carolyn.

"I agree," said Mom. "I'll give you three dollar bills for thirty dimes, dear. And I'll even contribute an envelope and the money you'll need for a stamp. You had better take your envelope to the post office and have it weighed. It might cost extra because of the two dimes in it."

"That'll be great, Mom," said Maryellen. "Three dollars and twenty cents isn't a fortune, but it's something, and—" She grinned at Dad, "something is always better than nothing."

"Hear, hear," said Dad.

Maryellen felt very efficient and grown-up as she paper-clipped the three dollar bills to a piece of paper and taped the two dimes underneath them. She wrote:

Dear March of Dimes,
    All my friends and I are so glad Dr. Salk found a polio
vaccine! Here is some money to buy shots for people,
especially children.
Sincerely yours,
Maryellen Larkin

She addressed the envelope to the local March of Dimes
headquarters in Daytona Beach, and it was ready to go.
Since the next day was Sunday, when the post office would
be closed, she would mail the money on Monday.

✳ ✳ ✳

On Monday, Maryellen hurried home from school. Mom
was making snacks for everyone when the phone rang.

Carolyn answered it. "Ellie, it's for you," she said, holding out the receiver. "It's some man."

Maryellen took the phone. "Hello?"

"Maryellen, this is Dr. Oser," the man said. "Today, five
children came to my office to be vaccinated against polio.
Their mothers said that the children had seen your show
and that's why they came to get their shots. So I'm calling
to thank you!"

"You're welcome," stammered Maryellen, a little shyly.

"One child brought a poster with him," Dr. Oser went
on. "It was one of the posters that you made to advertise

your show. I was wondering if you'd make another poster about getting vaccinated, so I could hang it up in my office."

"Me? You want a poster by *me*?" Maryellen squeaked.

"Yes, indeed," said Dr. Oser. "Bring it to my office in the Medical Building on Drayton Street whenever it's ready. I'd like to meet you."

"Well, okay, sure!" said Maryellen.

"Good," said Dr. Oser. "And thank you, Maryellen. You've done something important by encouraging these kids to get their shots. Good-bye."

"Bye," said Maryellen.

"Who was that?" asked Mom.

"It was a doctor who said that five kids got shots today because of our show," crowed Maryellen. "And he wants me to make another polio poster for his office."

"Holy cow!" exclaimed Carolyn.

"Ellie!" breathed Beverly. "You're *famous*."

Mom hugged Maryellen. "That's wonderful, sweetie," she said. "Dad and I are so proud of you! Off you go now, to the post office to mail your money."

"I'll come with you," said Carolyn.

"I want to go, too!" said Beverly.

Naturally, Tom and Mikey wanted to come, and that meant Scooter, too, so there was quite a crowd gathered behind Maryellen as she handed her envelope to the lady at the post office.

"Please, may I buy a stamp for this?" Maryellen asked politely.

"Sure, honey," said the lady behind the counter. She looked at the address. "March of Dimes, eh?"

"It was all Ellie's idea," said Beverly. "It was her birthday party. She put on a show to earn the money. She's ten now. And today a doctor called and said kids got polio shots because of her show, and he wants her to make a poster for his office."

"My word!" said the lady. "That's a very impressive contribution to our community. You should be proud of yourself, Miss—" she looked at the return address on the envelope in her hand—"Maryellen Larkin."

"Thank you," said Maryellen, pink in the face.

"No, thank you, Maryellen," said the lady. "It'll be an honor to mail this letter for you."

✳ ✳ ✳

A few days later, the phone rang. "I'll get it," Carolyn hollered. In a moment she called out, "Ellie, phone for you."

Maryellen thought it was probably Dr. Oser, so she was surprised when a high, fluty voice said, "Hello. Is this Miss Maryellen Larkin?"

"Uh, yes . . ." Maryellen hesitated. Then she snorted,

"Har-dee har, har, Wayne. Very funny." She was sure that it was Wayne, making a prank phone call in one of his silly voices. But why was Wayne calling her?

"Excuse me," said the voice, sounding even higher and flutier. "This is Betty Plotnick, the secretary for the mayor of Daytona Beach. Am I speaking to Miss Maryellen Larkin?"

"Cut it out, Wayne," said Maryellen. "Stop goofing around. I know it's you."

"No, this is Bet-ty Plot-nick," said the voice, pronouncing the words slowly. "I need to speak to Ma-ry-ell-en Lar-kin, please."

Suddenly it dawned on Maryellen that maybe it wasn't Wayne after all. "Oh, I'm sorry!" she sputtered, wishing that she could sink into a pit. "This is Maryellen."

"Good!" said the woman. "The mayor of Daytona Beach would like you to ride in the Memorial Day parade with him."

"Do what?" gasped Maryellen. "I mean, thank you! But why?"

"In recognition of your support for the March of Dimes," said Betty Plotnick. "The mayor's office has had three letters about you: one from a Dr. Ron Oser, one from Miss Evelyn Danziger of the U.S. Post Office, and one from a Mr. David Fenstermacher, who wrote to the March of

Dimes, and they forwarded his letter on to us."

"Davy wrote a letter?" asked Maryellen.

Betty Plotnick went on, "The mayor is impressed with your sense of responsibility and the fine example you set for the young people of our town. Please come to City Hall at eight a.m. on Memorial Day. Good-bye!"

Flying Machines
✳ Chapter 6 ✳

 oom, thumped the drums. *Toot-tootle-toot-toot,* blasted the trumpets. *Whoosh, snap, flap,* fluttered the flags in the warm Memorial Day morning breeze. "Hurray!" cheered the crowds lining the streets as Maryellen waved to them from the mayor's convertible.

It was easy not to have stage fright in the parade, because she didn't have to say anything. Even when the newspaper reporter had interviewed her before the parade, all she'd had to say was her name. The mayor told all the rest of the story about her show. Then the newspaper reporter took a photo of Maryellen and the mayor sitting in the convertible. On the sides of the convertible were signs that said:

Maryellen Larkin
Youngest March of Dimes Fund-Raiser
in Daytona Beach!

As the parade moved on, Maryellen could see the silvery flash of batons and the gold flash of cymbals up

"Hurray!" cheered the crowds as Maryellen
waved from the mayor's convertible.

ahead as the high school marching band led the way. Colorful balloons bobbed in the air, and people tossed confetti. There were a fleet of fire engines, floats decorated with crepe-paper flowers, a man dressed as Uncle Sam on stilts, and clowns riding tiny tricycles. Maryellen smiled and waved as she passed the reviewing stand, which was decked out in red-white-and-blue bunting.

Maryellen's smile grew even wider when she saw her family lined up along the street. Mikey was on Dad's shoulders, Mom held Tom up so that he could see, and Joan, Jerry, Carolyn, and Beverly stood all in a row. The Karens and Angela were there, too, and Davy and Wayne, all wildly waving little American flags.

"Hurray, Ellie!" they shouted. "Hurray, hurray, hurray!"

Waving to them, Maryellen thought there could be no happier ten-year-old than she was in the whole wide world.

✳ ✳ ✳

On the last day of school, the students could barely contain their exuberance. Mrs. Humphrey tried to keep the classroom quiet and orderly, but it was like trying to calm a herd of wild horses. When the class came in from recess, Wayne jumped up onto his chair and chanted, *"No more pencils! No more books! No more teachers' dirty looks!"*

"Ah, Wayne," sighed Mrs. Humphrey. "How I will miss you!" Everybody laughed, because they knew that

Mrs. Humphrey meant the exact opposite of what she had said. As the next period began, Mrs. Humphrey was clearly glad to turn the class over to Mr. Hagopian, one of the fifth-grade teachers.

Mr. Hagopian stepped forward and spoke to the class. "Because you are going to be in the fifth grade next year, you are eligible to be in the Science Club," Mr. Hagopian announced. "I hope you will join, because the Daytona Beach school district is sponsoring a science contest and our school is hosting it. Students can team up today and then meet about their projects over the summer. In the fall, the projects will be judged and the winners will be chosen." He paused for dramatic effect, and then said, "Students in the contest will invent a flying machine."

"Oooh," all the students murmured, as an electric current of excitement ran through the class. Recently, a rocket had been launched into outer space from Cape Canaveral, which was not far from Daytona Beach, so just about everybody was fascinated by the notion of rockets.

Wayne stood up and ruffled his hair and made his fingers into eyeglasses, pretending to be a mad-scientist-inventor, just as he had in Maryellen's polio show. "I vill vin!" he said in a fake accent.

Everyone laughed until Mr. Hagopian gave Wayne a withering frown.

Wayne meekly slid back down into his seat.

Mr. Hagopian went on, "All interested students are invited to meet in my classroom after lunch today."

Maryellen wished it were after lunch *already,* she felt so fired up about the contest!

With a gentle swoosh, a paper airplane landed on her desk. Maryellen knew it was from Davy. She turned around and grinned at him. Davy had always been interested in airplanes and things that fly, and Maryellen always loved a challenge to her imagination, so, without saying a word, they knew that they would both join the science club.

But at lunch, Maryellen's other friends had lots of words to say—mostly discouraging ones—when she announced, "I am so excited about the science contest!"

"Why on earth would you want to do an extra science project, of all things?" asked Karen King. "I mean, that's like giving yourself homework over the summer!"

"I *would* take part in the contest," said Karen Stohlman. The other three girls slid sideways glances at one another. They knew that Karen Stohlman liked to copy Maryellen. "But what with Girl Scout camp, swimming lessons, and ballet," Karen went on, "I'm going to be too busy."

"I think the contest sounds like fun," Angela said, "but I'm going to Italy to visit my relatives, so I won't be able to meet with a team over the summer. Maybe I'll join the club in the fall, though."

"Not me!" said Karen King. "Watch out, Ellie," she cautioned. "You're not going to know anybody in the club. Probably the only kids who will show up at the meeting today will be older boys."

"I bet that's right," agreed Karen Stohlman. "And they'll be drips who read science-fiction comic books."

Maryellen's enthusiasm wavered for a moment. She understood that the Karens were warning her that if she joined the Science Club, she would be regarded as strange. Most kids thought it was weird for girls to like science.

Just then, Davy tapped her on the shoulder. "Come on!" he said. He looked so excited that Maryellen's doubts disappeared.

"See you later!" she said to the Karens and Angela. As she jumped up from the lunch table to follow Davy, her enthusiasm was only slightly dimmed by the fact that Wayne, wearing his helicopter beanie, was glued to Davy's side, as always.

Maryellen was a little embarrassed to walk into Mr. Hagopian's fifth-grade classroom with Wayne spinning the propeller on his beanie, because she immediately saw that the Karens were right: Most of the kids were boys who were going to be in the sixth grade next fall. There were only two other girls there.

"Settle down, kids," said Mr. Hagopian. "Today, I'll divide you into teams. Your task at this first meeting is to brainstorm. Over the summer, you'll flesh out your ideas. Your team will choose the best idea and build your flying machine in the early fall, and then you'll be ready for the contest. Any questions?"

A big boy called out, "Is it true that the contest winners will be interviewed on television?"

Mr. Hagopian nodded. "I'm sure they will."

Well, thought Maryellen, *that settles it.* All her life she had dreamed of being on television! Now she was more excited than ever.

Mr. Hagopian divided the kids into two teams, and Maryellen found herself the only girl on a team with Davy, Wayne, and four older boys.

A tall boy named Skip immediately took control. "Okay, guys," he said, looking only at the other fifth-grade boys as if Maryellen, Davy, and Wayne were invisible. "Let's just save time and say I'm captain of our team. We'll call ourselves the Launchmen."

"Just a second," Maryellen protested. "Don't we get to vote or anything?" She looked around, but only Davy seemed to share her indignation at how bossy Skip was.

Skip glanced at Maryellen. "You take notes." He handed her a piece of paper. "Write on the back of this."

"Notes? But why . . ." Maryellen stammered, taken aback. It was bad enough that Skip had dismissed her—and Davy, too—lumping them together with helicopter-head Wayne as lowly still-really-fourth-graders. But by casting her in the supporting role of secretary, Skip made it seem as if she were not an equal member of the team but someone who was there only to record other people's ideas. "How come I have to take notes?"

"You're the girl," said Skip, as if the connection between being a girl and being a secretary was obvious.

"Well, that doesn't—" Maryellen began, but the Launchmen had already launched themselves into a loud conversation about their flying-machine ideas.

Maryellen sighed and looked at the paper that Skip had given her. At the top it said "Rules of the Contest." That sounded important. She began to read and as she did, she saw one rule in particular that she thought the rest of her team needed to know about. "Hey, guys!" she said. "You should—" But no one listened to her, so she gave up.

Maryellen loved to doodle, so as she listened to the boys pitch their ideas, she made sketches on the blank side of the rules sheet of what they were describing. She was quicker and better at sketching than at writing—her handwriting was never very good—and besides, she was not going to take notes, no matter what bossy Skip said.

"Let's make bird wings!" said one boy. "I'll strap 'em on and fly."

"No, let's make our flying machine in the shape of a football, and I'll throw it," said another boy, demonstrating his throwing arm.

"Let's build a kite, and then cut off the string when it's flying high," said Davy.

"That's baby stuff!" scoffed another boy. "Let's build a B-52 bomber!"

"Or a helicopter!" Wayne contributed, flicking the propeller on his beanie to make it spin and pretending to be lifted up.

"Wait, *what*?" said Maryellen, dismayed at how bad the ideas were. Davy's kite idea was the only idea that sounded the least bit practical. But the boys weren't listening to one another, so they certainly wouldn't listen to her.

Maryellen was relieved when Mr. Hagopian called out, "Okay, kids! Go back to your classrooms. Let's meet at the same time next week at the public library. See you then."

Maryellen folded the paper with the rules on one side and her sketches on the other and put it in her pocket. As she and Wayne and Davy headed back to Mrs. Humphrey's room, Davy asked, "How come you were so quiet in the meeting?"

Maryellen shrugged. "I did have a few ideas, but it seemed like if I suggested them, the big boys would shoot 'em down."

"I don't think any of their ideas will work," said Davy. "We've got to come up with better ideas if our rocket's going to take off."

"Taking off is only part of the contest," said Maryellen. "The winner has to stay in the air the longest. It's in the rules. If the Launchmen ignore the rules, they'll be the Loser-men for sure."

Westward Ho!

✳ Chapter 7 ✳

o celebrate the last day of school, Mom had set up the sprinkler in the front yard. Within minutes of being home from school, Maryellen and Beverly were in their bathing suits running through the deliciously cold sprinkler water. Tom and Mikey danced from foot to foot just at the edge of the spray, while Scooter watched from the shade.

Suddenly Beverly said, with wide eyes, "Look!"

Dad was turning in to their driveway, and attached to his car was a huge silver trailer. Dad honked the car horn, and Mom, Joan, and Carolyn came dashing out of the house. As Dad got out of the car, Tom and Mikey ran to greet him.

"What on earth is *that*?" asked Mom when everyone had settled down a bit.

"Isn't it a beauty?" said Dad, patting the trailer proudly.

"It's the 1955 Airstream. And it's all ours. We are going to see the U.S.A. this summer, kids, and this will be our home away from home."

"Hurray!" cheered everyone but Mom.

"We're taking a family road trip," said Dad. "It'll be a chance for some real togetherness. I thought we'd head out west, to Yellowstone National Park."

"I love the idea of heading west!" Maryellen gushed. "Just about all my favorite TV shows are Westerns!" Maryellen pictured herself riding a galloping horse across the sagebrush prairie, sleeping out under the stars, and crossing raging rivers like the pioneers. "Please can we go to the Alamo, Dad?" she begged. "Davy Crockett was there." Maryellen and the little kids sang the song from the TV show:

Davy, Davy Crockett!
King of the wild frontier!

"Davy Crockett?" sniffed Joan. "I can't believe you idolize a guy who walked around with a dead raccoon on his head. I think *all* those Westerns you love so much are ridiculous."

"They are not," Maryellen protested. "You—"
But Mom held up both hands to stop them. She looked

harried. "I've got Joan and Jerry's wedding breathing down my neck," she said to Dad. "There's still so much to do. The painters are coming next week to get the house ready for the wedding. Who'll supervise them—Scooter?"

"Scooter will come with us," said Dad. "And don't you think you'd like a vacation from all the wedding worries?"

"I don't think it *will* be a vacation for me," said Mom. "Driving cross-country in a trailer just means I'll do all my usual work under tougher-than-usual conditions. It also means we won't see my parents this summer."

Everyone was quiet, thinking about what Mom had said. Maryellen could see that Mom had several valid points.

"Mom," said Maryellen, "what if Grandmom and Grandpop came *here*? That way, we could see them, and they could take care of the house while we're gone and be sure the painters are doing everything right. They could stay for a while after our trip, too, so that we could have a nice long visit together."

Mom considered her suggestion. "That might work," she said, nodding and smiling a little.

"That's a great idea, Ellie," said Dad, beaming.

Maryellen turned eagerly to Mom. "And I'll take care of Scooter on the trip, I promise." Truthfully, she didn't think that being responsible for lazy, sleepy Scooter would be

very hard. She added, "And I'll help
with other chores, too." Cleaning
the tidy trailer would be a breeze!

"I'll help, too," said Carolyn.
"It'll be *fun* to keep the Airstream
nice and neat and shipshape."

"You needn't worry about cooking much, sweetheart," said Dad to
Mom. "We'll mostly be eating the fish I catch. I'll fry 'em
up over a campfire."

"And you can teach Joan to cook in the little Airstream
kitchen, and then *she* can make dinner for us, too," added
Maryellen.

"All right," said Mom. She shrugged in surrender.
"Westward ho, I guess."

✳ ✳ ✳

The next few days were a hurricane of shopping,
packing, gathering, and preparing. Dad bought a tent and
sleeping bags at the Army Navy store because there were
not enough beds for everyone in the Airstream. Mom went
to the grocery store to buy food for the trip. "In case the
fish aren't biting," she said, winking at Dad.

Jerry, Joan's fiancé, drove the girls in his hot rod to the
library to stock up on books. On the way home, he stopped
at a diner and generously treated everyone to French fries

and ketchup. Joan had to eat her French fries with one hand, because Jerry was holding her other hand, the one with the engagement ring on it.

"I'm going to miss you," said Jerry to Joan. "I wish you didn't have to go."

Beverly giggled. "Mushy!" Maryellen kicked her leg under the table to shush her.

Joan sighed. "I don't really want to, but Dad has his heart set on this being a whole-family trip. I can't let him down."

"You'll have lots of time to read, anyway," said Jerry. "I know how you love books." He smiled and squeezed Joan's hand. "I'm a lucky guy, marrying a girl with brains *and* beauty."

Joan put her French fry hand on top of Jerry's. "I'll be thinking of you and missing you every mile of the way," she said, and the look Jerry gave her was so sweetly romantic that Maryellen and Carolyn practically swooned.

✳ ✳ ✳

This land is your land, this land is my land,
From California to the New York Island,
From the redwood forest, to the Gulf Stream waters,
This land was made for you and me!

Maryellen, Carolyn, and Beverly sang nice and loud, and Mom and Dad did, too. Tom and Mikey didn't know the words, so they just hollered, "My land!" whenever they felt like it. Only Joan maintained an aloof silence. Mile after mile she gazed out the open window at the passing countryside looking very mournful and lovelorn.

"What's the matter with Joan?" asked Beverly in a whisper when they stopped for lunch on the third day.

"I think she just really doesn't want to be on this trip," said Maryellen.

"Yeah," agreed Carolyn. "It seems like the farther away she gets from Jerry, the mopier she is."

Even though it was crowded in the backseat, the rest of the kids had fun in the car. They sang and played car games like finding all the letters of the alphabet in order on the signs that they passed. Signs for Burma-Shave shaving cream were the best, because they had *u* and *v*, and in the correct order, too. Everyone loved to read aloud the funny poems, which were divided on six separate signs that advertised Burma-Shave. Maryellen's favorite went,

> *She kissed*
> *The hairbrush*
> *By mistake*
> *She thought it was*
> *Her husband Jake*
> *Burma-Shave*

✶ ✶ ✶

One night after dinner, Maryellen was sitting on a rock by the fire with Scooter at her feet and her sketchbook in her lap. Joan was next to her, reading by firelight.

Carolyn added a log to the fire and then asked, "Can I see what you're drawing, Ellie?"

"Sure," said Maryellen. She scooted over so that Carolyn could share the rock.

"Airplanes, birds, bees, leaves, clouds, kites, and sparks," said Carolyn. "You've sketched just about everything that goes up in the air."

"Yup," said Maryellen. "I'm hoping I can show those Launchmen boys, especially that bossy Skip, that girls have good ideas, too."

Suddenly Joan surprised Maryellen and Carolyn by saying, "Emily Dickinson has a poem that begins, 'Hope is the thing with feathers.'"

Carolyn smiled at Maryellen. "So keep your hopes flying high!"

"I'll try," said Maryellen. She turned to Joan. "I guess you're hoping this trip will be over soon so you can get back home and marry Jerry."

A funny look—wistful and unsure—slipped across Joan's face. Then she looked down at her book again. "Mmm," was all she said.

✳ ✳ ✳

Mom and Dad were very fair: Everyone in the family had an equal vote on where they should stop and what attractions they'd visit. When Maryellen said they should visit the Alamo, Beverly, Tom, Mikey, and good-natured Carolyn went along. Joan groaned, but she was outvoted. The Larkins would always remember the Alamo, because that's where tempers began to get short and Dad's idea of togetherness turned into falling-apartness for Joan and Maryellen.

When they got to the Alamo, Joan separated herself from the rest of the family and walked around the fort alone looking moody. But Maryellen loved being at the Alamo. She said to Carolyn, "Gosh, it gives me goose bumps to be where such a famous person as Davy Crockett actually was. Maybe he touched this very wall, or walked this very walkway, or slept in this very room where we are right now." She had a sudden, wonderful thought. "Maybe, if I become as famous as Davy Crockett, people will come tour *our* house sometime in the future."

"Maybe!" said Carolyn cheerfully. She turned to Joan, who had wandered over to them. "Whaddya think, Joan?"

Joan looked thoughtful, and then she said briskly, "I think I'm going to the gift shop to buy a postcard to send to Jerry."

Joan left. Carolyn and Maryellen rolled their eyes at each other. "It's as if she's not really on this trip with the rest of us at all," said Maryellen.

Relations between Maryellen and Joan were no better when they returned to the Airstream. Maryellen was conscientiously trying to do her job of caring for Scooter. Tonight, like every night, while Mom tried to teach Joan how to prepare dinner, Maryellen filled Scooter's dog-food bowl and then sang the Chow-Chow Dog Food jingle to call Scooter to dinner. The jingle went to the tune of "Twinkle, Twinkle, Little Star." Maryellen sang:

> *Chow-Chow Dog Food,*
> *Eat it up,*
> *And you'll be a*
> *Happy pup!*

"You're driving me crazy with that song," Joan complained to Maryellen, looking up from scouring a pan she'd burned. "It's stuck in my head!"

"Sor-ree!" said Maryellen. But she wasn't, really. She and Scooter liked the song. In fact, Maryellen made a point of humming the tune as Scooter ate his dinner.

Fireworks
* Chapter 8 *

After the Alamo, the Larkins drove north and west. Maryellen rolled down the window and let the wind whip her hair as she admired the view. She thought back to school, with Mrs. Humphrey at the piano leading the class in a rousing rendition of "America the Beautiful." Maryellen always belted out the lyrics with gusto:

> *O beautiful for spacious skies,*
> *For amber waves of grain,*
> *For purple mountain majesties*
> *Above the fruited plain!*

But it wasn't until now, driving across America with her family, that Maryellen really understood what the words meant. The skies above Nebraska truly were spacious, the vast fields of grain in Kansas really did look like golden waves in a windswept ocean, and the mountains in Wyoming were purple as they rose up against the horizon.

Joan might be longing for home, but Maryellen wasn't.

She loved seeing the country with her own eyes. *Yes,* she thought, *America **is** beautiful.*

✳ ✳ ✳

"Now, kids," said Dad when they got to Yellowstone National Park, "you are about to see one of the wonders of the world. It's a geyser called Old Faithful. Stand back and pay attention."

At first, nothing happened. Then, from a hole in the ground, water and steam burbled up. Next, water sprayed up like a fountain, until—*whoosh!*—the geyser shot up into the air as tall as a skyscraper in a spectacular explosion of scalding hot water, spray, and steam that shook the earth beneath their feet.

"*Whoa!*" gasped Maryellen and Beverly, clutching each other as the crowd applauded the geyser.

Maryellen tilted her head back to see the top of the geyser against the blue sky. *If a geyser of water was lifting something and holding it aloft, would that count as a flying machine?* She gazed at it in wonder as the shaft erupted in a column for nearly five minutes and then sank lower, lower, lower, until it disappeared, hissing, back into the ground.

At the campground, Dad unhitched the Airstream. He

drove the station wagon around Grand Loop Road so that everyone could see elk, buffalo, and bears. They hiked to the Grand Canyon of the Yellowstone, and they walked near the hot springs that burbled up out of the ground, holding their noses to block the sulfurous smell.

When they returned to the Airstream, Mom had to hurry and make dinner, and after dinner, when the rest of the family went to hear a ranger talk about stargazing, Mom stayed at the campground to put Mikey to bed and tidy up the trailer. Mom didn't grumble about it, but Maryellen could see that Mom's prediction had come true: The trip was hard work for her. Mom was trying to teach Joan how to cook, and Joan was trying to learn so that she'd know how to cook for Jerry after they were married. But everything that Joan cooked turned out the same way: burned black. Hamburgers, cookies, pancakes, baked potatoes, and fried eggs all became hockey pucks because Joan would get so distracted by whatever book she was reading that she'd forget what she was cooking until smoke filled the Airstream. So Mom had to be vigilantly on cooking duty most nights.

Even Dad was sort of letting Mom down. Fish turned out to be harder to catch than Dad had expected, so Mom had to come up with something for dinner even after long days of hiking.

Maryellen tried to be very conscientious and keep her promise about caring for Scooter. She walked Scooter around the campground every morning. Even though it was a chore, it was fun. Everyone was friendly, and everyone loved Scooter, who had very good manners for a dog.

One afternoon, as the Larkins arrived back at their trailer after a hike to see mud pots and waterfalls, Dad announced, "It's the Fourth of July, so tonight there's going to be a barbecue with music and square dancing at Old Faithful Lodge. After that, we'll drive outside the park to see some fireworks!"

"Hurray!" cheered the kids.

"I love fireworks!" Maryellen exclaimed.

"I know you do, honey, but Scooter does not," said Mom. "Someone has to stay behind in the trailer with Scooter tonight to keep him calm, and since Scooter is your responsibility, Ellie, I think you are that someone."

"I'll stay, too," said Joan. "I want to wash my hair and iron a blouse."

"Watch out," Carolyn whispered to Maryellen. "Don't let Joan fry her blouse as if it's a grilled cheese sandwich."

Maryellen mustered a smile, but after the rest of the family had left, she felt like Cinderella stuck at home while everyone else went to the ball, even though in this case it was a square dance. It was hard to be cheerful as she sang

Scooter's come-to-dinner song:

> *Chow-Chow Dog Food,*
> *Eat it up,*
> *And you'll be a*
> *Happy pup!*

"Ellie!" Joan said, sounding testy. "Would you please stop singing that song? It's so annoying. Scooter is, too, the way he slobbers over his dinner."

"Okay, okay!" snapped Maryellen. She gave Scooter an extra helping of dog food to make up for Joan's mean words about him.

When it got dark, Maryellen looked out the windows of the Airstream. She could hear fireworks in the distance, but the windows were too small and the trees were too big for her to see them. She sighed with frustration and boredom. She slid her eyes sideways to look at Scooter, who was snoozing under a bed and so deeply asleep that he looked as though nothing could wake him, not even if a loud firecracker went off right next to him.

Grabbing her notebook, Maryellen pushed open the door and went outside. Now she could see the fireworks high in the sky. Some blossomed like giant chrysanthemums, or like dandelions blown apart by a puff of wind.

Others looked like squiggles, or jet streams, or silvery star showers. Some shot straight up, like Old Faithful. Others looked like multicolored snowflakes that dissolved into shiny streams of blue, green, red, and gold as they fell toward earth.

As she began to sketch, Maryellen noticed that some of the fireworks went off all at once in one tremendous burst, and others went off in stages, climbing higher in the sky with each burst. First there was one explosion, then another explosion higher up than the first, and then a third explosion that was highest of all. Each part boosted the next, Maryellen realized, and that's why they stayed in the sky the longest.

Wait a second, she thought, her heart thumping. *That's it—booster rockets!* Her team should make their flying machine in parts, each part pushing up the next. That was how to keep it in the air longer!

Maryellen was so excited, she suddenly felt as if the fireworks were celebrating with her as they lit up the whole sky. Then *rat-a-tat-rat-a-tat-tat!* An incredibly loud string of firecrackers exploded, and *zoom!* Scooter burst out of the trailer, bolted past Maryellen, and disappeared into the dark.

"Oh no!" wailed Maryellen. "Scooter! Come back, boy!" She dropped her sketchbook, ran around the outside of the Airstream, and flung herself onto the ground, trying to see if Scooter was underneath the trailer. "Scooter, I know you're scared. Come on out, *please.*"

But Scooter was not there. He was gone, swallowed up by the night.

"Ellie, what are you shouting about?" asked Joan, just out of the shower.

"It's Scooter," said Maryellen in a shaky voice. "He ran off. It's all my fault. I was distracted—thinking about my flying machine and sketching the fireworks—and I opened the door, and someone set off firecrackers, and Scooter bolted out and took off and—"

"Calm down," interrupted Joan. "He can't have gone

far. Just rattle his bag of dog food and call him. He'll come."

"No, he's gone," Maryellen insisted. "Please, Joan, you've got to help me find him before he gets eaten by a bear, or sucked into one of those smelly mud pots, or falls over a waterfall."

"Oh, all right," said Joan. "You get the flashlight while I get dressed. Get a map of the park, too."

"Thank you, Joan," said Maryellen.

"Go!" said Joan, bossily shooing Maryellen. "And find some bandannas or something to use as a bandage, in case Scooter is cut or scratched."

The light from the flashlight bounced along the pine-needly path as Maryellen and Joan set out to search for Scooter. They went to every tent or trailer in the camp-ground to ask if anyone had seen him. Most people had gone to the party at the lodge, but those still at the camp-ground all knew and liked Scooter because he was such a friendly dog, and they promised to keep an eye out for him.

One man, who was rather well padded himself, said, "Who'd have thought fat old Scooter could run fast or far? He's such a tub of lard."

Maryellen was surprised and pleased when Joan stiffened and said tartly, "Guess we shouldn't judge by appearances, should we?"

I never thought I'd see Joan stick up for Scooter, Maryellen thought. *Maybe she really does like Scooter after all.*

A young woman by the shower house said that she'd seen Scooter running out of the campground a little while ago. "He went that way," she said, pointing off into the darkness.

"Thanks," said Maryellen. She peered at the map. "Oh no," she groaned. "Scooter is headed toward Yellowstone Canyon! What if he falls into the Firehole River and gets swept away by the rapids?"

"Stop it," said Joan firmly. "That sort of talk won't help." She tapped the map. "Look. There's a ranger station in that same direction. We'll go tell them our dog is missing. We can look for Scooter on the way there."

"Okay," said Maryellen. At times like this, she was glad that Joan was bossy.

Disaster!

* Chapter 9 *

The girls walked in silence, following the small circle of light that Maryellen's flashlight made on the path. Surrounding them was utter, solid darkness.

Suddenly, Joan grabbed Maryellen's shoulder. "What's that panting sound?" Joan whispered. "What if it's a bear or a mountain lion following us?"

"Maybe it's Scooter!" said Maryellen. She swung the flashlight around them, but all she could see were tall trees. She held her breath and listened, and then said, "I think you just heard me breathing hard. But if you're worried about wild animals, we should sing really loud. That will scare them away."

"You're kidding," said Joan. "Where'd you learn *that*?"

"Television," said Maryellen. "Probably on one of those cowboy shows that I like so much and you *dis*like so much."

Joan laughed. "I know a song we can sing really loud," she said. She began to sing, *"Davy, Davy Crockett..."*

And Maryellen joined in: *"King of the wild frontier!"*

After singing a few more television theme songs, Joan

said, "Did we make a wrong turn? I thought we'd see the ranger station by now."

"Me, too," said Maryellen. "Let's go back to that fork in the path."

By now, they were in such deep woods that they couldn't see the sky. Joan led the way, and Maryellen kept the light shining by their feet so that they wouldn't trip over tree roots or rocks in the path. She was just thinking how she wished she'd worn jeans instead of a dress, since low branches were scratching her legs, when she thought she heard a rushing sound like cars on a highway, except of course there were no cars or highways nearby. *Must be the wind in the trees,* she thought, *or a river.* She gasped. *A river?*

"Hey, Joan," Maryellen said. "Wait—"

But she was too late. One second Joan was there, walking right in front of her, and the next second Maryellen heard a thump and an anguished scream. Joan had disappeared.

"*Joan!*" shrieked Maryellen.

"Help!" came the muffled reply. "Ellie, help!"

"Where are you?" cried Maryellen, frantically shining the flashlight all around her but seeing only pine trees.

"I don't know," wailed Joan. "I just stepped off into nowhere. I've fallen off the path somehow. Hurry up.

But don't do what I did. Be careful!"

Maryellen dropped onto her stomach. She slithered forward like a snake, slowly swinging the flashlight from side to side. She was so scared and shaky that the light from the flashlight was jiggly. Suddenly, she came to a sharp drop-off. The path collapsed into a washout that fell to the rushing river below.

"I can see your light," called Joan. "I'm down here."

Maryellen tilted the flashlight down, and there was Joan, about six feet down in the darkness. She was holding on to a tree root with one hand and balancing on one foot on a rock that stuck out from the steep hillside. She was too far down for Maryellen to reach with her hands.

"Hang on," said Maryellen. She sat up and pulled the bandanna off her head. She tied it to the bandannas she'd stuffed in her pockets and then dangled them over the ledge like a rope. "Can you grab this?" she asked.

"Of course not," said Joan, sounding impatient. "First of all, I can't even see it because it's pitch black down here. Secondly, I'm too heavy. I'd pull you down here, and then we'd be worse off than ever. Think of something else."

"Okay," said Maryellen. This time, she tied the end of the bandanna rope around the flashlight handle, and then dangled the flashlight over the edge. "Can you climb toward the light?" she asked.

*She tied the end of the bandanna rope around the flashlight
handle, and then dangled the flashlight over the edge.*

"Yes, I think so," said Joan. "It's lighting the way for me."

Maryellen could hear Joan breathing hard as she scrabbled up the vertical incline using rocks and roots as toeholds and handholds until at last, with an *oooph,* Joan dragged herself over the lip. Maryellen grabbed Joan by the seat of her pants and hauled her all the way up onto flat ground.

For a second, both girls huffed and panted. Then Joan said, "Thanks, Ellie-kins." Joan stood up, but winced. "Oh no. I think I sprained my ankle in the fall." She tested putting weight on her foot. "*Ow, ow, ow,*" she said.

Maryellen found two sticks and put one on either side of Joan's ankle as splints. She wrapped her bandannas around the sticks and the ankle and tied the bandannas tightly. Then she found a tall, thick stick with a notch at the top and gave it to Joan. "Here, use this as a crutch," she said.

"Jeez Louise, Ellie," said Joan, almost laughing. "Where'd you learn how to do all this rescue and first aid stuff? Girl Scouts?"

Maryellen shook her head. "On the Davy Crockett show, people are always falling off cliffs or slipping into quicksand and spraining their ankles and stuff. I've always liked pretending I'm Davy, rescuing somebody."

Joan snorted. "Okay, so maybe that guy with the dead raccoon on his head is not so useless after all," she said. She gave Maryellen a little hug with her free arm, and then left it across Maryellen's shoulders to lean on her as they walked.

"We'd better just go back to the campground," said Maryellen. "We can try again to find Scooter when it's light out."

Joan nodded. Maryellen could tell that it took all of her strength to keep going because she tensed with every step.

"Listen, Joan," Maryellen said. "I'm sorry about all this."

"All what?" asked Joan.

Maryellen sighed. "Well, I know that you think Scooter is a pain. And now, because I wasn't paying attention to him, Scooter is lost and you've got a sprained ankle. What a disaster."

"It is a disaster, isn't it?" said Joan. To Maryellen's surprise, she chuckled. "You know what, though? It's weird, but I kind of like it. It's like an adventure in a book." She squeezed Maryellen's shoulder. "Or a TV show."

"Well, shtick with me, shweetheart," Maryellen joked, trying to sound like Humphrey Bogart in the movies. "I can get you into all the disasters you'd ever want!" Then, turning serious, she asked, "You mean you aren't even sorrier to be on this trip? You don't hate it even more now?"

Joan sighed. "I don't hate this trip," she said.

"Then how come you've been so distracted and moody?" asked Maryellen. "Haven't you been staring out the car window, missing Jerry and wishing you were home?"

"I do miss Jerry," said Joan. "But when I'm staring out the car window, I'm just trying to drink it all in. It's as if every house and town that we pass is a book, and I'm curious about its story. I even found the Alamo interesting. That's why I wanted to walk around it alone."

"Really?" asked Maryellen, amazed. She and Carolyn had completely misunderstood Joan! "If you like the trip, why haven't you said so?"

"Well," said Joan, taking a deep breath, "partly because I didn't want to admit that I was wrong. And partly because I would have felt disloyal to Jerry." She paused, and then said, "Ellie, I'm all mixed up, and I'm afraid I've sort of taken it out on you and Scooter. I'm sorry. See, this trip has made me realize that the world is a great big fascinating place. If I've seemed distracted and moody, it's because I . . ." Joan wavered, and then she blurted out, "I'm questioning my decision to get married."

Maryellen stopped abruptly. "What?" she gasped.

"I love Jerry," said Joan quickly, "and I love the idea of living with him. Even though so far," she joked, "a fire extinguisher seems to be the kitchen utensil I use the most, so we'll starve if he can't cook."

"That's true," said Maryellen with a chuckle. "So do you have any idea what you want to do?"

"Well, yes," said Joan. "And actually, you are the one who gave me the idea."

"I did?" said Maryellen. "What idea?"

"Remember at the Alamo, when you were saying how exciting it was to be where Davy Crockett had really been?" said Joan. "You made me think how I'd love to go to Massachusetts and see where my favorite poet, Emily Dickinson, lived. And I've always wanted to see the home of Louisa May Alcott, who wrote *Little Women*, and see Thoreau's Walden Pond. And then there's New York City. Lots of writers lived there, and London, and Paris . . . Ellie, I want to travel and visit the places where all the writers that I love have lived. I want to go to college and study the books they've written. And then I want to help other people love those books and writers as much as I do, maybe by becoming a teacher."

"Oh," said Maryellen, thinking hard. She and Joan walked in silence for a bit. Finally she asked, "Do you have to choose between Jerry and college? Can't you have both? I mean, you can still go to college if you're married, right? And the same goes for traveling. Maybe

Jerry would like to travel, too. Have you ever asked him?"

"No," said Joan slowly. "No, I haven't. But I will. I sure will as soon as we get home." With the arm that was not on the crutch, Joan reached over and hugged Maryellen. "You have great ideas, Ellie. Thanks."

Just then, a twig snapped in the dark woods beside the path. Maryellen and Joan stopped still and clutched each other.

"Quick, let's sing," said Joan.

"I'm too tired," said Maryellen. "I can't even think of a song."

"I can," said Joan. Her voice was very loud, and only quavered a little as she sang,

> *Chow-Chow Dog Food,*
> *Eat it up,*
> *And you'll be a*
> *Happy pup!*

Rustle, rustle, crack. Something was slithering toward them through the underbrush, coming closer and closer. Joan and Maryellen held their breath, and the wild animal stalking them swaggered out onto the path.

Home Sweet Home

✳ *Chapter 10* ✳

I t was Scooter!
Both girls dropped
to their knees—Joan very
gingerly—and hugged him.
"Scooter!" they cried with joy.

"Oh, I am so glad to see you!"
said Maryellen.

Joan even kissed Scooter on his nose. "Where have you
been?" she chided him. "You scared us to death!"

Scooter remained calm. He acted as if causing more
excitement than the Fourth of July fireworks was all in the
course of a perfectly normal day for him. He yawned as
Joan used her crutch to struggle to her feet, and he gra-
ciously allowed Maryellen to carry him all the way back to
the campground.

Maryellen, Scooter, and Joan had not been back long
before the rest of the Larkins returned from the fireworks.

"All quiet here on the home front?" asked Dad.

Maryellen and Joan lifted their eyebrows at each other.

"Not exactly," said Maryellen. "It was all my fault,

really," she confessed. "You see—"

But Joan interrupted. "*I'll* tell what happened," she said, in her good old bossy way.

So Joan told the whole story of Scooter's disappearance, summing it up with, "Ellie is a real hero. She was brave and knew just what to do."

"Does this mean that you will help Ellie take care of Scooter from now on?" asked Mom with a twinkle in her eye.

"Uh, no," said Joan swiftly. "Not entirely, that is. But there's one thing I can do—help her call him to dinner!"

Scooter howled as the whole family sang,

> *Chow-Chow Dog Food,*
> *Eat it up,*
> *And you'll be a*
> *Happy pup!*

✳ ✳ ✳

Joan's ankle healed quickly, and all the way home across the country from Wyoming to Florida, she held true to her promise. Every evening, she helped Maryellen summon Scooter to dinner, whistling along while Maryellen sang the dog-food song. Sometimes Joan winked at Maryellen while she whistled, in silent acknowledgment of the conversation they'd had in the woods. Maryellen felt grown-up to be the only one who knew Joan's secret hopes and dreams and ambitions. She was pleased to have this special bond with Joan. They even had their own private theme song!

Nevertheless, even Maryellen was pretty tired of the Chow-Chow Dog Food song by the time Dad pulled into their driveway. They all climbed out of the car feeling stiff and sweaty and very glad to be home.

"Welcome back!" said Grandmom as she gathered Beverly, Tom, and Mikey in a big hug. Grandpop hugged Carolyn and Maryellen.

Jerry was there to greet Joan. He scooped her up in a hug, too—a hug that was only for her. "Did you miss me?" he asked.

"I sure did," said Joan. "Oh, I have so much to tell you!"

Maryellen caught Joan's eye and smiled.

"Home sweet home," Mom sang out. She put her hands on her hips and said to Dad with semi-pretend exasperation, "I'm glad to be here, even if I do have to put up with this gigantic silver spaceship parked in our driveway. I feel as if I'm living at Cape Canaveral."

"Now, honey—" Dad began.

But Grandpop interrupted. "Come tell me about all the fish you caught," he said to Dad, and off the two men went.

✳ ✳ ✳

"I've never been so excited for the first day of school,"
Maryellen said to Davy a few days later. She skipped
a skip of happiness as they walked to school together.
Her booster-rocket idea boosted her confidence: She was
sure that now the Launchmen would listen to her and be
impressed with her brainstorm. "When's the first meeting
of the Science Club?"

"Not till next week," said Davy. "Don't worry, you
didn't miss much at the summer meetings. We still don't
have a good idea for a flying machine."

"I do," said Maryellen. "Well, I have part of an idea."

"What is it?" asked Davy.

Before she could answer, Wayne screeched up from
behind them on his bike, the propeller on his beanie hat
spinning wildly. He slammed on his brakes to make his
bike skid sideways right in front of Maryellen so that she
had to stop short. "Greetings, earthlings," he said in a flat
voice like a robot.

Maryellen sighed. *Here we go,* she thought, *starting
another school year with zany Wayne.* To Davy she said, "I'll
tell you my idea later." She didn't want to say anything in
front of Wayne because she was sure that he'd blab her idea
to everyone in the Science Club before she had a chance
to present it. It was hard not to tell Davy, though. She felt
almost as if she had fireworks with booster rockets going

off inside herself. She was positive that good old Davy would share her enthusiasm.

Before classes began, Principal Carey announced over the PA system that the new fifth-graders should meet in the auditorium. When everyone gathered, Principal Carey made a startling announcement. "Our school building is so crowded that it is bursting at the seams," he said. "So to use our space efficiently, and to improve academic performance, we'll now have 'pullout groups.' Some students will be pulled out of their homeroom classrooms and sent to different teachers for math and English."

Everybody knew that meant they were being separated by ability, and the smartest kids would all be in the same pullout groups. As the day went on, the girls found out that Angela and Maryellen were in the top math group, but the Karens were not. Maryellen and Karen King were in the top English class, but Angela and Karen Stohlman were not.

When the girls met at lunch, Karen King lifted her milk carton to toast Maryellen, saying, "Congratulations on being chosen for both of the top pullout groups, Ellie."

"Oh," said Maryellen, "thanks."

Karen Stohlman sighed. "I liked it better when we were all in the same class. Now that we're in different groups, we won't see one another as much as we used to."

"Let's be together every chance we get, like at lunch and recess," said Angela. "I'm going to be a Girl Scout this year, so we'll be together at meetings. And our new homeroom teacher, Miss Martinez, is starting a baton-twirling club. We could all join that."

"Yes! Good idea!" said the Karens.

"I don't think I can join anything else new," Maryellen said slowly. "I just joined the Science Club."

"Oh," said Angela, crestfallen. "Right."

"What if the Science Club meets at the same time as Girl Scouts?" asked Karen Stohlman. "Which one will you choose?"

"Well, I...uh," Maryellen stumbled over her words. "I'm pretty excited about the science contest. I drew lots of sketches over the summer, and I have a really good idea for a flying machine. So, I guess...I guess I'd choose the Science Club."

Maryellen's friends were quiet. The silence was awkward, weighed down with hurt feelings. Finally, Karen King said, "Gee, Ellie, it seems like it's more important to you to be in the Science Club than it is to be our friend."

"No!" Maryellen protested. "That's not true!" She felt terrible. Was it selfish of her to hurt and disappoint her friends? Was she wrong to go off on her own? She wrapped up the rest of her sandwich and put it back in her lunch bag. Her throat was so tight she knew she couldn't swallow another bite.

✳ ✳ ✳

That afternoon, the air was so soupy that it was hard to breathe. So after school, Maryellen and Carolyn walked the little kids down to the beach. Joan was already there, camped out comfortably under a beach umbrella, reading.

"Hi, Joan," they said.

"Hi," she answered, not looking up from her book.

The kids tossed their towels next to Joan and stampeded across the sand and into the water.

Maryellen plunged headfirst under the first giant wave coming toward her and heard it thunder above her and crash behind her onto the shore. She bobbed up, blinking in the glaring sunlight that bounced off the water, and grinned. As usual, the ocean refreshed her. Nobody could feel hot and bothered or grumpy-grouchy-gloomy in the ocean! She could see Carolyn playing with Beverly, Tom, and Mikey, splashing in the shallow water, and she could hear them laughing and shouting with glee as the water tickled their legs.

After a while, Maryellen strolled back up the beach to Joan's umbrella and flopped onto the sand.

Joan looked up. "How was your first day of school?"

"Not so good," said Maryellen.

"How come?" asked Joan.

"Well, the Karens and Angela have hurt feelings because I'm staying in the Science Club, which means we won't see each other as much," Maryellen explained.

"Why are you staying in the Science Club?" asked Joan. "I thought you said that those sixth-grade boys were annoying."

"They are," sighed Maryellen. "But I just really love the idea of inventing a flying machine."

"Well, I think if you love something, you have to stick to it and stand up for it," said Joan. "Even if it doesn't make sense to other people, or isn't what they expect you to do. If you love it, do it."

"Is that how you feel about reading?" Maryellen asked.

"Yes. I love reading," said Joan with a contented sigh. "I love books more than anything."

"More than Jerry?" asked Maryellen curiously.

Joan replied slowly, "Noooo."

"Is it a tie?" asked Maryellen.

"Mm-hmm," said Joan. She made an apologetic face and nodded. "I'm afraid it is."

"Why're you afraid?" asked Maryellen. "It's not as if

you have to choose between Jerry and books. You can have both, can't you? Have you spoken to Jerry about going to college yet?"

"Yes," said Joan. "And he thinks it's a great idea for me to go—someday. But right now we can't afford it. See, because Jerry was in the Navy in the Korean War, he's been living in the dorm and taking classes free of charge. The GI Bill pays for returning veterans to go to college. But married students have to live in married-student housing, and even though the rent is low and Jerry and I will both be working part-time, we can't afford rent and tuition for me."

"If only you could live somewhere for free," said Carolyn, who had joined them under the umbrella and was helping Mikey dry off while Beverly helped Tom. "You could live in our house, but it'd be awfully crowded. Some of us would have to sleep in the carport."

"Or in the tent we took on our trip," said Beverly.

"Hey," said Maryellen, bursting with a brainstorm. "How about the Airstream? You and Jerry could live in the Airstream! It could be your home sweet home!"

Get To It!

* Chapter 11 *

L ive in the Airstream and pay no rent!" crowed
Carolyn. "That's brilliant."

"I want to live in the Airstream, too," said Tom.

"Me, too," said Mikey.

"Just think, Joan," said Maryellen enthusiastically. "You
could park the Airstream by the college most of the time,
and then if you wanted to travel and Dad wasn't using
it, you could hitch it to Jerry's hot rod and off you'd go!
You could drive up to Massachusetts to see where those
authors you like lived. And Mom'll be thrilled to get the
Airstream—the 'gigantic silver spaceship' as she calls
it—out of the driveway, and Dad'll be thrilled that she's
thrilled. You'll be doing both of them a favor."

Joan's face brightened with hope momentarily, but then
she shook her head. "Oh Ellie, it's cute of you to come up
with such a wild idea, but it's too much to ask Mom and
Dad to let Jerry and me take over the Airstream," said Joan,
"especially with all the expenses of the wedding coming
up." She sighed a sigh from the bottom of her heart. "The
truth is, I think they might have to sell the Airstream to

pay for my wedding, even though Jerry and I don't want
a big hoopla. But Mom's mailing the invitations tomorrow.
After that, there'll be no turning back."

"But you do want to get married, right?" Maryellen
asked.

"Yes," Joan said. "But the fancy, formal wedding Mom
has planned is so . . . so different from what we want."

"What do you want?" asked Beverly simply.

"You mean besides not making Mom unhappy?" asked
Joan.

"Yes," said the other girls.

Joan spoke earnestly. "I'd like to be married right in
our backyard, with just our families around us. Nothing
big, nothing fancy, nothing to distract us from the most
important thing, which is Jerry and me promising to love
each other and take care of each other forever." She smiled.
"Then we'd celebrate with a little party."

"Cake," said Mikey happily. Though he was young, he
knew what was important at a party.

"Oh, right, Mikey honey," said Joan, giving him a swift
hug. "Maybe cupcakes!"

Maryellen stood up and brushed the sand off her
knees. "Okay, then," she said briskly. "Let's get to it."

"Get to what?" asked Joan.

"Your wedding," said Maryellen. "Saturday's the day

after tomorrow. I think we can have everything ready by then."

"No, we . . . I mean, but . . ." Joan sputtered. "A surprise backyard wedding? I just couldn't do that to Mom. She'd be so disappointed! She has her heart set on what she thinks of as a perfect wedding."

"Mom just wants you to be happy," said Carolyn. "She'll understand."

"Besides, Mom has five other children," Beverly pointed out. "So she has lots more chances at perfect weddings."

"And didn't you just tell me that if you really love something, you have to stick to it and stand up for it?" said Maryellen. "Didn't you just say that if something is right for you, then you should do it even if it doesn't make sense to other people?"

"Yes, but—" Joan began.

"So your wedding won't be the way other people do it," Maryellen continued. "It'll be the way you and Jerry do it. It'll be perfect for you."

"I guess so," said Joan, a bit dazed.

"Do we still get to wear our bridesmaid dresses?" asked Beverly.

"Of course," said Joan.

"And your bride outfit is ready, all except the veil," said Maryellen.

"You can wear a tutu on your head, like Wayne did after Ellie's show," joked Carolyn.

"I was thinking maybe just a flower," laughed Joan. She looked at them all and smiled exuberantly. "You know what? Nobody ever had better brothers and sisters than I do. You're helping me make my hopes and dreams come true. Thanks a million, you guys!"

✳ ✳ ✳

On her wedding day, Joan wore a cream-colored gardenia tucked behind her ear. Afterward, everyone agreed that Joan was the most beautiful bride they'd ever seen and that Joan and Jerry's backyard wedding was the most beautiful—and *relaxed*—wedding they'd ever been to. Beverly, Maryellen, and Carolyn wore their glamorous bridesmaid dresses, finished by Mrs. Fenstermacher and Grandmom. Joan and Dad—and Mom, too, at Joan's insistence—walked down a pathway lined with buckets of jasmine and hibiscus toward Jerry and the minister. Maryellen thought that Jerry looked movie-star handsome in his white Navy uniform, and he didn't look at all stiff or formal; he had a smile a mile wide!

After the ceremony, all the guests were given white balloons, white kites, white paper fans, and white tissue-paper flowers. They ate cake (Mom insisted on making a traditional multilayered cake) and ice cream cones (Joan's

idea) and strawberries on toothpicks. The kids flew their kites, running around the backyard. Mikey fell asleep with frosting on his face. Beverly and Tom got a big kick out of blowing up the extra balloons and then letting them go so that they spiraled around crazily, making a wonderfully rude noise as they deflated: *Pfffft.*

"This," sighed Joan to Maryellen as they surveyed the sunny scene, "is exactly what I wanted." Just then, a deflating balloon *pffffft*ed its way over to the patio and landed in

Dad's lemonade, and Joan and Maryellen laughed.

Joan and Jerry drove off in Jerry's hot rod, trailing the Airstream behind them. Their honeymoon was only going to be the rest of the weekend, because Joan had an interview on Monday with the college admissions office to see if she could enroll in January. But even though the honeymoon was going to be short, Maryellen, Carolyn, and Beverly had thoroughly decorated the back of the Airstream anyway, with a big sign that read, "JUST MARRIED," and a string of old shoes and tin cans tied to the bumper.

"Good-bye, good-bye," everyone called, and Joan and Jerry drove off in a shower of flower petals.

Dad put his arm around Mom, who was sniffling. "Aw, sweetheart," Dad said comfortingly, "don't be sad. Kids grow up. That's just what they do."

"I'm not sad," Mom said. "I'm crying tears of joy because I'm so glad to get that spaceship out of the driveway!"

But as Mom dabbed her eyes with a hankie, Maryellen could tell that was only half true. She understood. Her own heart was happy for Joan but sad at the thought of what it would be like without Joan in the house. There would be an empty space in their family. Even though Joan and Jerry would be nearby, and visit often, Maryellen knew that nothing would ever be quite the same again.

✳ ✳ ✳

The very next day, Florida's September rainy season began with grim determination. "Thank goodness it didn't rain like this on Saturday," said Mom on Monday, as Maryellen got ready for school. "We'd have had to move the wedding into the carport." As it was, in a dry corner of the carport there were leftovers from the wedding— grounded kites, un-blown-up balloons, crumpled fans, a partly used box of toothpicks, and drooping tissue-paper flowers—that had been hastily tossed into a box.

Maryellen glanced at them as she opened her umbrella and stepped into the wet, gusty wind. Normally, she would be dying to tell her school friends all about Joan's wedding. But after their difficult conversation last Thursday, they had avoided one another on Friday. Would her friends still be upset with her? Maryellen wasn't sure she wanted to find out.

Because it was raining, the students gathered in the gym before school started rather than outside on the playground as usual. It was hot in the gym. Maryellen unbuttoned her raincoat and flapped the two sides to cool herself off.

"Good idea," said Angela, appearing at her side with the two Karens.

"Yeah," said Karen King. "I feel like a steamed lobster."

The girls smiled at one another a little sheepishly, and finally Karen Stohlman said, "Listen, Ellie, we're sorry for being so snippy last week."

"Yes," said Angela. "Especially if we're not going to see each other very much, we need to be nice to each other when we do, right?"

"Right," said the Karens and Maryellen.

"Hey," said Angela. "I hear your sister had a surprise wedding on Saturday."

"She did!" said Maryellen. "In our backyard."

"Oh, I think that is the most romantic idea I ever heard," said Karen Stohlman.

"Tell us everything," begged Karen King.

By the time Maryellen had described the wedding in detail, it was time for school to begin. The girls went their separate ways to their separate classes, and Maryellen was relieved that they'd settled their differences so unfussily.

Later, when they met for lunch, it was only the teeniest bit awkward as the Karens and Angela talked about their Girl Scout meeting to be held that day after school.

"Did you forget to wear your Girl Scout uniform, Ellie?" Karen King asked. Angela jabbed her and frowned. "Oh. Oh, *right*," Karen said quickly. "Your Science Club meets today. I forgot. Well, uh, that'll be fun."

"I hope so," said Maryellen. "Anyway, thanks for not being upset with me anymore about it."

"Well," said Karen Stohlman philosophically, "we're in the fifth grade now. We're more mature than we were in fourth grade, so we're smarter about how dumb it is to fight."

"Yeah," said Karen King. "Plus, we get it that all of us like to do different things. But as long as we still like each other, that's all that matters, right?"

"Right!" agreed the four girls, Maryellen most heartily of all.

Maryellen Takes Off

* Chapter 12 *

aryellen immediately saw that Davy was correct: She hadn't missed much by not being at the Science Club meetings over the summer. The two other girls had dropped out. The Launchmen were all talking at once, launching their ideas forcefully at one another as if the ideas were ballistic missiles.

"Hey!" said Maryellen to her teammates.

Everyone ignored her.

Maryellen smacked the desk with her sketchbook. "HEY!" she said again. This time the boys stopped talking and looked at her. "The contest is in two weeks. Don't you think we'd better get a plan?"

"We've got a plan," said Skip, full of swagger. "My plan." He spread a crinkly piece of paper on the desk. It was covered with smudged sketches.

"Well, even if your plan is good," said Davy, "we should look at other people's, too."

"Davy's right," said Maryellen. "We should discuss everybody's ideas."

"Nope. Waste of time," said Skip.

"You can't just boss and bully us into using your plan, Skip," said Maryellen. She thought about how Mom and Joan had listened to each other with respect and made compromises so that the wedding pleased them both. "Maybe the best idea will be a combination of lots of different people's ideas."

But unlike Mom, Skip was a tyrant. "Who asked you?" he said. "You never even came to the summer meetings."

"It's not in the rules that you have to come to every meeting," said Maryellen. "The rules—"

"Let's just build Skip's machine and stop whining about the rules," urged a tall boy.

"Have you even *read* the rules?" asked Maryellen, pulling the paper with the rules on it out of her sketchbook. "If you had, you'd know the contest isn't a race. It isn't about speed; it's about time. The flying machine that stays up in the air the longest wins."

All the Launchmen—except Davy and Maryellen—frowned.

"I tried to tell you guys during the summer," said Davy, "but you wouldn't listen."

"Give me that," ordered Skip. After he looked at the rules, he tossed the paper back to Maryellen and crossed his arms over his chest, saying, "So, what's your idea, genius?"

Everyone looked at Maryellen. Except for Davy, they all had expressions of distrust and doubt on their faces.

"Look," she said. She held up her sketchbook to show the Launchmen. "When I was on vacation, I saw fireworks, and I noticed that the fireworks that stayed up in the sky the longest went off in stages. Each explosion lifted the next part higher. So my idea is to use booster rockets to lift the different parts of our flying machine."

"How will the parts connect?" asked one boy.

"Well, I don't know," said Maryellen. "But—"

"How'll they blast off from each other? How'll they know *when* to blast off from each other?" asked another boy.

"I don't know," said Maryellen again, "I—"

"What'll provide the power to make any of it fly up in the first place?" asked another boy.

"I'm not sure yet," said Maryellen. "I thought we'd figure it out together, as a team. I was thinking maybe it could be powered by water. You know, like water out of a squirt gun."

"A squirt gun?" several kids repeated with scornful disbelief. Others howled with laughter, as if she had said something hilariously stupid.

Skip exhaled with exasperation. "First of all, shooting something up with water will never work," he said, counting off on his fingers. "Second, your whole stages and boosters idea stinks. Third, we don't need a dumb fourth-grade girl to tell us what to do. Got it?"

Maryellen felt a blazing red-hot flash of fury shoot up her spine. She remembered how Joan said that you have to stand up for what you love. *That's true flipped around, too,* Maryellen thought. *Sometimes you have to stand up against what you hate.* Quietly, she shut her sketchbook and, without saying a word, gathered her belongings to leave. As she stood up, so did Davy.

"Hey, Skip," said Davy. He counted off on his fingers. "First of all, you're a bully. Second, Ellie's idea of stages doesn't stink. Third, we're in the *fifth* grade, and we don't need a stuck-up sixth-grade boy to tell us what to do. Got it?"

"Yeah!" said Wayne. He flicked the propeller on his beanie to make it spin, and then he and Davy followed Maryellen out the door.

❋ ❋ ❋

"Did you yell like when you quit your birthday-party polio show?" asked Karen King. It was still raining, so the girls were in the gym the next morning, waiting for classes to begin. Maryellen had told her friends how she and Davy and Wayne were no longer Launchmen. "Did you storm out and slam the door?"

"No," said Maryellen, blushing. She felt embarrassed recalling the temper tantrum she'd thrown when she quit the polio show. She had learned from that experience that it's better to stand up for yourself without making a spectacle of yourself.

"You changed your mind about quitting the polio show," said Angela. "Do you think you might change your mind and go back to the Launchmen?"

"No," said Maryellen again, remembering how they had laughed at her and dismissed her for being younger—and a girl.

"You were so excited about planning your flying machine," said Karen Stohlman kindly. "You drew all those sketches in your sketchbook. It's a shame to waste all that work. Does it say in the rules that you have to be on a team? I mean, couldn't you make a flying machine and enter it in the contest by yourself?"

"Fly solo," Karen King piped up.

"I don't think it's against the rules," said Maryellen. "But I also don't think I can make the flying machine all by myself. I need help. I don't even have a complete idea yet. And I'd also need help to fly the machine at the contest."

"We'll help you," said Angela immediately.

"Really?" asked Maryellen.

"Sure!" said Karen King. "Even if we're not all that interested in flying machines, you're our friend and you want this, so we do, too. The four of us will make our own new team."

"And I bet Davy will help us if we ask him," said Karen Stohlman.

"We should ask Wayne, too," said Maryellen. "After all, he stood up for me."

"Way-ay-ay-ne," sighed Karen Stohlman. The four girls rolled their eyes at one another at the thought of working with Wayne.

"We're trying to make something that'll fly, right?"

said Maryellen, feeling happy and lighthearted. "So maybe it'll be useful to have Wayne on our team. He's a *bird*brain! Get it?"

The girls giggled and flapped their arms like pretend wings as they headed off to class.

At lunch, Karen Stohlman reported that Mr. Hagopian had said it was fine to form a new team. Maryellen reported that she had invited Davy and Wayne to join the team, and the boys had said yes right away.

So the newest Science Club team met in the Larkins' carport on Saturday afternoon. Naturally, Mikey, Tom, and Beverly came out to see what was going on, but they soon lost interest in the team's conversation and began scrounging around in the box of wedding leftovers. Mikey, who was under the impression that they were having another wedding, handed everyone a tissue-paper flower, or a kite, or a fan. Beverly and Tom found a bag of balloons. They blew them up and then let them go to careen around wildly and make the same rude noise they'd made at Joan's wedding: *Pfffft.*

Wayne was enchanted. He ditched the team meeting to join Beverly and Tom. Since Wayne was bigger than they were, he could blow his balloon up so that it was bigger and flew longer. The rude noise Wayne's balloons made was louder and even more disgusting than Beverly's and

Tom's, especially when he used one of the long, hot dog–shaped balloons.

When one of Wayne's *pfffft*ing balloons smacked Karen Stohlman in the forehead, she said, "Cut it out, Wayne."

But Maryellen smacked her own forehead with the palm of her hand. "That's it—a balloon! Air squirting out of a deflating balloon will provide the power to lift our flying machine."

Davy looked at the kite and the tissue-paper flower Mikey had given him. "I wonder if we could make a tiny little kite out of tissue paper and toothpicks," he mused, "and attach it to the balloon."

"And after the balloon loses all its air, the kite will still fly for a while," said Karen Stohlman, "so our machine will stay up longer."

"Well," said Karen King, who never let enthusiasm get in the way of constructive criticism, "I don't think one balloon will have enough power to lift even a little kite very high."

Everyone had to admit that this was probably true.

"How about more than one balloon, then?" asked Angela. "How about two?"

"Good idea," said Maryellen, starting to sketch.

Wayne surprised everyone by speaking up. "I still really like Ellie's idea of booster rockets," he said.

"Thanks, Wayne," said Maryellen. "What if we blow up three balloons, and attach the kite to the middle balloon? We clip the side balloons shut and use a rubber band to shut the middle balloon and connect it to the side balloons. When we're ready to launch, we unclip the two side balloons, and they take off. When they deflate, the rubber band falls off, so the middle balloon takes off. When it starts to descend, the kite will slow its fall, like a parachute would."

Everyone crowded together to look at Maryellen's sketch. For a while, no one said anything, and she held her breath in nervousness and hope. Finally, Davy said slowly, "I get it. The side balloons are the first stage, the middle balloon is the second stage, and the kite is the third stage, even though all it does is glide. Let's try it."

"Good job, Ellie," said Karen Stohlman.

"Oh," said Maryellen, "I may have drawn the sketches, but everybody supplied the ideas. Our whole team did a good job."

"We are a good team," said Karen King. "We really should have a name."

"How about the Loony Balloonies?" suggested Davy.

"That's it!" said the Karens and Angela and Wayne—who celebrated by sending another balloon *pfffft*ing around the carport.

The Loony Balloonies
* Chapter 13 *

y lips are dead," moaned Karen Stohlman. "I think I must have blown up a million balloons."

"Wayne, if you shoot one more rubber band at me, I'll handcuff your hands together with it," snapped Karen King.

It was a week later, and the Loony Balloonies were gathered again in the Larkins' carport. They had soon realized that a plan on paper and an actual flying machine that really flew in real life were two very different things. Sometimes the balloons popped. Sometimes the kite fell off. Sometimes the rubber band was too tight. Sometimes the clips were too loose.

They worked all afternoon. Angela was endlessly patient about gluing the tissue paper to the toothpicks to make the tiny kites, and Davy was best at attaching them to the balloons. Karen Stohlman blew up balloon after balloon after balloon. When they needed metal clips and glue, Wayne sped off on his bike and fetched them quickly. Karen King was tireless at spotting problems and pointing out mistakes. And just when everyone was so tired and discouraged that they were about to quit and go home in defeat, Maryellen cheered them up and made them laugh by tossing scraps of white tissue paper into the air and pretending it was snowing.

Now it was practically dinnertime, and at last, the team finally felt sure they had figured out how to construct a three-stage, balloon-powered, tissue-paper-kite flying machine that worked reliably. The carport was strewn with balloons and broken toothpicks and bits of white tissue paper. But after hours of experimenting and improving and trying again and again, the team was prepared for the contest, which was taking place the next Saturday.

"I think we're ready," said Maryellen optimistically.

"Well, we're as ready as we'll ever be," said Karen King. "It'll either fly or it won't."

✳ ✳ ✳

The day of the science contest was bright and clear. The Loony Balloonies stood in a silent cluster, looking at all the other teams lining up on the field preparing their very impressive flying machines. Davy spoke for the whole team when he said with genuine concern, "Wow."

"Yeah," said Karen King. "I didn't realize we'd be competing against rocket ships. Some of these gizmos look like they could fly to the moon, for Pete's sake."

"Come on," said Maryellen briskly. "Let's get ready." She led her friends to set up their flying machine as far away from the Launchmen as possible—all the way across the playground. Even so, from that distance, Maryellen and her team could see and hear the Launchmen all talking at once and no one listening to what anyone else had to say.

"Our machine may not work better than theirs," said Angela. "But our team sure does."

Angela turned out to be wrong. The balloon-powered, tissue-paper-kite flying machine worked *better* than the Launchmen's plane. When Davy took the clips off, the two booster balloons effortlessly lifted the middle balloon high into the sky.

Maryellen tilted her head back and shaded her eyes. She felt as if her heart was flying up, too. When the booster balloons deflated and the rubber band loosened so that the middle balloon took off, the Loony Balloonies whooped  and hollered happily. Soon the middle balloon was out of air and began wafting down to earth, but the little kite attached to it slowed its descent so that it swooped and spiraled in a gentle drift, finally landing in the grass with a whisper. Wayne ran to pick it up off the ground and held it above his head, and the whole crowd cheered loudly. Maryellen noticed with satisfaction that the Launchmen clapped, even Skip, though he clapped in slow motion.

The Loony Balloonies did not win the contest; a team from another school won with a three-foot-long rocket powered by gasoline. But the crowd cheered again, even louder than the first time, when Mr. Hagopian announced, "The judges have decided to award a special prize for creativity to . . ." He paused, then turned and beamed at Maryellen's team, "the Loony Balloonies!"

Maryellen was so surprised that she just stood there with her mouth open while the Karens and Angela hugged her with such force that, if she had been a balloon, she would have popped.

"Nice job!" said Mr. Hagopian, congratulating Maryellen's team after the applause ended.

"Thanks," said Maryellen, still a bit stunned. "I didn't even know there was a prize for creativity."

"There wasn't," smiled Mr. Hagopian. "We made it up on the spot, just for your team, because we thought you were so clever to have a machine with several stages. And we were impressed with the creative way you used simple materials to construct your machine."

"It was all stuff left over from my sister Joan's wedding," said Maryellen.

"But it took real creativity to figure out how to put it all together to make a flying machine," said Mr. Hagopian.

Some reporters and photographers came over to

interview Mr. Hagopian. Maryellen and her team stood quietly watching as a TV reporter asked Mr. Hagopian questions and then held a microphone up to his mouth as he answered, while a TV camera whirred, filming it all.

When they had finished interviewing Mr. Hagopian, one of the newspaper photographers said to Maryellen, "Hey, I remember you. Aren't you the girl I photographed last May in the Memorial Day parade, riding with the mayor?"

"Yes," said Maryellen. Suddenly, she was aware that the TV camera was pointed toward her.

"What's your name, miss?" asked the TV reporter. "And why were you in the parade?" Maryellen hesitated shyly.

"She's Maryellen Larkin!" said Karen Stohlman.

"She was in the parade because she put on a show to raise money to fight polio," added Karen King.

"Why are you all here today?" asked the TV reporter.

Davy spoke up. "We entered the flying-machine contest," he said. "Thanks to Ellie, we won a special prize for creativity."

"And if there had been a prize for having the most fun, we'd have won that, too!" said Angela. All the Loony Balloonies murmured in happy agreement.

"So, Miss Maryellen Larkin," said the TV reporter. "You are a girl with good ideas for flying machines and for helping people. What is the most important idea you learned from this contest?" He pointed his microphone right at Maryellen, so she had to answer all alone.

She thought for a moment. "Well, you know, our flying machine was made up of ordinary things like balloons and rubber bands—not the kind of things you might expect a flying machine to be made of," she said. "But every part was equally important. Every part had its own job to do to make the machine fly." She grinned. "And it was the same with the Loony Balloonies. Our team was made up of different people who are good at different things. But every person was equally important, because to make the machine fly, we needed all those different things. It wouldn't have worked if we hadn't included everybody."

Maryellen paused and as she did, she looked at good old Davy, her funny, faithful friends the Karens and Angela, and zany Wayne. Then she went on, "I guess what I learned is that different is good. Just because an idea isn't what people expect, you shouldn't ignore it. In fact, the best ideas come when you're *not* trying to be like everybody else."

"Ah," said the reporter. "I see. What you're saying is that each one of us is an individual, and we contribute our unique abilities to the benefit of the group as a whole. So the most important thing that a team needs to do to succeed is—?"

"Listen," said Maryellen immediately. "Listen to each other. Because every idea deserves respect, and every person does, too."

✳ ✳ ✳

That evening, all the Larkins were in the living room watching TV when the local news came on. Everyone cheered and then shushed one another when the segment about the science contest began. First the TV reporter interviewed the winners of the contest, and they explained how their rocket worked. Then the TV reporter said, "Now I'd like you to meet Miss Maryellen Larkin, whose team won the creativity prize."

And there was Maryellen, on TV, right in her own living room and in living rooms all over Florida.

As Maryellen, surrounded by her family, watched herself on TV surrounded by her friends—the Karens, Angela, Davy, and Wayne—she could hardly believe that what she was seeing was real. How long had she dreamed of being on television? But as she watched, Maryellen realized that this was even better than what she had dreamed of for so long. Because the great thing was that she was on TV as herself. She wasn't an imaginary character in an imaginary episode of an imaginary adventure. She was her own true, regular old self. In fact, that was *why* she was on TV, because she was who she was: the one and only Maryellen Larkin.

Inside Maryellen's World

Maryellen's story is fiction, but it was inspired by real events. In 1954, polio was a terrible threat. The disease, which usually struck children, often started like the flu, with a fever, aches, and weakness, but it could last many months and could cripple or even kill the patient. There was no cure, so patients were kept in isolation wards, away from their families, until they recovered. No wonder Maryellen remembered her illness as a dark, frightening time. When the vaccine was announced to be safe and effective, people wept with joy as church bells rang and car horns honked in celebration. Still, some parents feared the vaccine could make their children sick. So doctors promoted the vaccine, with great success. Since 1980, the U.S. has been polio free.

Kids raised money for polio by putting on shows, just as Maryellen does for her birthday. The hula hoop was new in 1958, so these children are showing off their hula hoop skills!

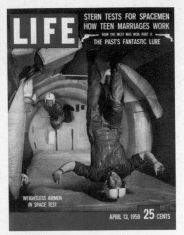

STERN TESTS FOR SPACEMEN
HOW TEEN MARRIAGES WORK
HOW THE WEST WAS WON PART II
THE PAST'S FANTASTIC LURE

WEIGHTLESS AIRMEN
IN SPACE TEST

APRIL 13, 1959 **25** CENTS

Trends featured in this 1959 magazine are astronauts and teen marriages. Like Joan, many young women in the 1950s married right after high school.

The 1950s brought other scientific advances that changed the world. In 1955, the U.S. government began a project to launch a man-made satellite into orbit, and the "space race" was on. Schoolchildren formed rocket clubs and competed to build flying machines, just as Maryellen does. When Russia launched its own rocket, *Sputnik*, in 1957, America stepped up its efforts. In 1958, a small satellite, *Vanguard 1*, was finally launched from Cape Canaveral, Florida. Today it's the oldest man-made satellite still orbiting the Earth!

Along with new discoveries in science and medicine, Americans were also discovering their country. By the 1950s, most families had cars, and popular TV shows like *Davy Crockett* made them want to see the real "Wild West." So they began taking trips to see Yellowstone and other western parks, just like the Larkin family.

Advances in health care and a booming economy made the 1950s a good time to be a kid— especially if you were in a

A busload of tourists admires bears in a national park.

Travel agencies appealed to families' interest in driving trips and outdoor recreation.

middle-class white family. If you were a member of a minority, life was more difficult. In the South, where the Larkins lived, African Americans were *segregated*, or kept separate from, whites. It was hard for black families to travel, because many hotels and restaurants refused to serve them. Black children went to schools that were supposed to be "separate but equal"—but the reality was that the black schools had less money and often not enough books or desks for their students. Linda Brown, an eight-year-old girl growing up in a racially mixed community in Topeka, Kansas, tried to enroll in the neighborhood school with her white friends, but the school board sent her to a black school farther away. So her father sued. The case, *Brown v. Board of Education*, went to the Supreme Court, which held that segregation was harmful and unconstitutional and must end. This decision became a landmark in the civil rights movement, which gained momentum during the 1950s and would soon bring even bigger changes.

Linda Brown's segregated classroom, above. A mother and her daughter celebrate the Supreme Court decision, right.

a Nez Perce girl who loves daring adventures on horseback

a Jewish girl with a secret ambition to be an actress

who joins the war effort when Hawaii is attacked

whose big ideas get her into trouble—but also save the day

who finds the strength to lift her voice for those who can't

who fights for the right to play on the boys' basketball team